Amaretto with *Coffee*

Jonah Bradford
Imports a Family

ALEXANDER D. BANYAN

Printed in the United States of America.

ISBN: 978-1-4907-1264-2 (sc)
ISBN: 978-1-4907-1266-6 (hc)
ISBN: 978-1-4907-1265-9 (e)

Library of Congress Control Number: 2013915153

Trafford rev. 08/22/2013

   www.trafford.com

North America & international
toll-free: 1 888 232 4444 (USA & Canada)
fax: 812 355 4082

Dedicated to my late friend, Michigan.

I will let him remain nameless, as he would have insisted.

*Michigan, as I called him in this book, had come to
my rescue more than once in the real world.
My life had become busy and complicated.
When I tried to find, Michigan, I discovered that he
had been called to another military mission out of the
country, and had died from cancer after his return.*

*A few of you, know his name.
Do not allow your lives to become so
complicated as to lose your friends.
We do not make that many true friends in this life.*

A. D. Banyan

Chapter 1

I was sitting in my sailboat at the galley table, staring at the laptop screen. I had failed to put any more words on the page. It was 92 degrees on deck and the air conditioner hummed in the background. I was listening to a few men on the dock that . . . *thought they were alone.*

"The money is in the master cabin. I have to lay low until Thursday and then we can meet Captain Raymond's boy out on the mooring buoys and do the transfer." Said a skinny man with long hair.

"What's this one worth?" Said his heavyset black friend.

"Eight hundred thousand dollars," He said quietly, "I told him I had it all in cash, this time!"

I figured out that they were working on a big drug deal, and I went up the galley way steps until I could see over the cabin. They were standing directly in front of my sailboat and I could see them clearly. I watched through the dodger glass where I felt invisible. The skinny man had a lot of tattoos on his body including one on his arm that was in color and said, *"Death from above."* There was a helicopter above it with the front shaped like a skull.

A breeze blew through the marina. A powerboat rocked my 50' mast. My bare foot slipped off of the tread master covered step and I instinctively caught myself by grabbing the edge of the cabin top. My hand made a loud slap as it pounded against the fiberglass.

The men froze and looked at me. I ducked back down into the cabin and stood silent with my hands on the Nav Station desk. I stood, considering calling the police, but decided that since they know who I am, I better just mind my own business. They walked away talking quietly and I sat back down at my computer. I was on E-Dock and I watched them as discretely as I could from below deck. They walked up the marina sidewalk to A-dock and went out to a large Nordhaven Trawler on the end. They stood on the bridge and looked at my boat with binoculars. I was very uncomfortable. I stayed below, and continued working on my book.

A few hours later I looked toward their boat and they either were below deck or had left. I took this as a good time to head back to my house. I gathered my laptop and headed for my truck.

"Jonah! Where are you going? Some of us are going to have a few drinks over at the Tiki Shack under the bridge. I was hoping you would go with *me*." Said Annie.

"Ohhh Annie . . . . I would love to . . . but tonight, I have things to do at home."

"Would you like some help . . . *at home?*" She asked quietly.

"I don't think *your*, help will get this manuscript finished. This is a PG book." Jonah joked.

"Let me know when you are back to writing *adult*, books. Bye!" Said Annie.

Annie is a few years older than I am. She has red hair, lots of freckles, and big green eyes that get her anything she wants. We are not in love. I'm not even sure we like each other that much, but if either one of us have a need . . . we take care of each other. We use . . . each other, and enjoy it. She was a visiting cruiser, two years ago, that decided she liked it here, and stayed.

*　　*　　*

I stayed home for the next few days. I mowed my grass, cut a lot of dead branches from my palm trees, and hauled it all to the dump in my Nissan pickup.

Wednesday evening I got bored. I decided to take the laptop and go back to the sailboat and work on my book some more. *(Some people have an office)* I always have fresh ideas, and sleep better, on the water.

I stopped on the way and picked up a bag of chips and a six-pack of Heineken. With the truck safely parked under a parking lot light near the marina office, I sat and looked out at the boats. With the laptop case on my shoulder, the grocery bag in one hand and a six-pack in the other, I proceeded to my boat.

"Hello Captain! *They are at it again!* We're leaving!" Said Russ, as I passed him and Rudder, *his black Lab,* on the dock.

I have a combination lock on the storage compartment in the cockpit and keep the key to the cabin inside it on a hook. I unlocked the companionway door and put the beer into the fridge. It was a busy night here. The live-aboards were all having a group barbeque, and one man with his young family was angry because of the foul language from a group of retired vets that had reached their limit. His noisy dog barked at them as their volume increased.

I still could not think with all the commotion, so I turned on the flat panel TV, lay back, and opened Heineken #1.

I turned off the 11:00 news and tried to sleep in the main cabin. The marina was refusing to die down. Now someone was screaming for them to:

"*SHUT UP! SHUT UP!!!*" as a self-proclaimed country singer bellowed it out over his houseboat PA speakers. I finally surrendered, packed up my computer, and left the beer in the cooler for another night. I shut off all the electric and turned the air conditioner up to 80 deg. I locked it all back up and walked toward the truck. I detoured past the marina restroom to recycle the beer and stood at the urinal.

The two men from the trawler came in and stood behind me.

"So . . . . What a you type'n on that puter?" He asked.

"Hell!!! Charlie!!! He don't type nothing! He just cruises the porno sites and jack'n off in his fancy sailboat!"

"Thanks you piece a shit!" Said Charlie, "Now he knows my name!"

He grabbed my shoulders and pushed me toward the door.

"We know you heard us on the dock!" Charlie said, "I hope you didn't have a hot date tonight, cause you're gonna stand er up!"

The black man pulled a revolver from under his shirt and crammed it against my ribs.

"We're gonna take a nice quiet walk aren't we partner?" Said Charlie.

"It does seem that way." I said, as I picked up my laptop and let them escort me down the dock.

Even as a hostage I was impressed with the Nordhaven. The chine of the hull was immaculate and the dark blue paint flaunted it proudly. The interior was immaculately finished and the control area would require a computer class to leave the dock. Only drug people and politicians could afford a boat like this.

"Keep walk'n! Yer almost home!" As he pushed me into a small cabin with bunk beds. My computer hit the floor as I caught myself against the bed. He locked the door with a key. I crawled onto the bottom bunk and started my laptop.

"All Right!" I thought, "It still works!"

I searched for internet access. Internet access was only available by paying in the marina office, and no one was using a router that I could get into. I shut it down and saved the battery for any future opportunity. As I explored the cabin for a weapon, the motors started and they relocated the boat to the public mooring field. They found a buoy off by itself and tied on.

The cabin was a small crew cabin and the only possible exit was the cabin door. I could have easily pried it open with the handle of the fire extinguisher, but Gook was stationed in the main cabin. I could tell that he would not hesitate to kill me if I tried. Killing me now, would actually be easier for them then explaining their complication when the delivery arrives. With an escape not being an option at this time, I lay in the bunk and listened.

They got louder, and I could hear them talking on deck, as they drank Jack Daniels. I slept on and off in the bunk and did a lot of thinking about my impending future.

About 2AM I was awakened by the sound of another boat with a deep rumbling sound. They kept the engines idling as they tied on to the side of the trawler. There were men on the other boat speaking Spanish and they all worked on moving the drugs from that boat, into the Nordhaven. It got quiet. Everything must have been transferred, and the money had changed hands. Through the porthole, I saw Charlie hand the fat brief case to the Colombian man in the speedboat.

I figured that, now that the deal was done, they would probably tie me up in *my* boat. They would move the drugs down the Intercostal Waterway to Miami, and the money would probably be destined for South Carolina. Later I could get out of my cabin and have no evidence of their existence.

"Gook!!! Get the Captain out a the cabin and move him over," Said Charlie.

Gook held a gun to my back and walked me off of the trawler, onto the speedboat, and back down into another locked v-berth cabin. I heard them talking about how much I had seen and heard and that I could even identify them!"

"Hey Boss! Here's his computer. I don't want anything link'n me ta him left on my boat!" as he handed it to the man on the speedboat.

$$*\quad*\quad*$$

I listened to the roaring of the motors for hours and finally drifted off, only to be awakened by the engines slowing down. I

Alexander D. Banyan

felt the wake from behind us hit the stern and lift the hull. One of the men came below and drug me up on deck. The boss was sitting in the cockpit going through my laptop.

"So . . . . You're a writer?"

"Yes." I said, as I was pushed into a seat.

He looked at me with respect and admiration.

"Such a waste."

He shut down my laptop and closed the screen.

"You don't need this anymore!" as he held it over the side.

"NO!" I screamed, as he laughed and pulled it back in.

"Please! That is how I make my living. All my books are in there!"

He stood and walked toward me and slapped the laptop against my chest as his man tied it to me with what looked like a . . . *clothesline.* They stood me on the dive platform of the transom and I balanced myself with the computer strapped to my chest. I glanced to the east to see a bit of my last sunrise. They gave the boat full throttle and I fell into the bubbling ocean. I went straight to the bottom and much to my surprise the bottom was only about thirty feet. I lie in the sand pulling at the soft rope that held my hands. Being wet, it had a bit more stretch and I got my hands free. I scooted the other ropes over my head as my laptop hit the sand. I shot to the surface and gasped for air as I watched the boat roar into the distance.

I had no idea where I was and there was no land in sight. I tried to guess at where the bottom would be this shallow, based on the time that had passed. I estimated from the glow of the sunrise in the distance that we had traveled south instead of north as I anticipated. The computer was trash but I dove back down and got it anyway. I can get a reflection of the sun off of the screen if I see another boat. I floated for hours on my back and kicked my feet as I slowly moved to the west. I estimated that I was somewhere east of Jupiter, and then I laughed at how crazy that sounded.

I may as well be *"A little East of Jupiter!"* I thought, as I looked at the big empty ocean.

6

The laptop was too heavy, so after trying to turn it on . . . . *just in case* . . . . I broke the monitor off and tucked it under my belt. All of my books, photos, and sacred information drifted to the bottom as I drifted a bit longer.

As the sun climbed higher over the water, I saw a commercial fishing boat coming in my direction. He was far enough away that I could just barely hear his motors running. I started flashing the monitor, as he got closer. After almost giving up and calling him several colorful things, he turned, and headed straight for me.

*   *   *

"Thanks for picking me up!" I said, as I leaned against the inside wall of his cabin.

He made me a sandwich and got me a bottle of water. "I think you will survive. Now, I have a business to run and time is money."

He turned and yelled out to his crew.

"Get those lines baited! Let's get these guys in the water!"

I lay back on the bench and went to sleep. I must have slept for hours. When I woke up, they were under way with several big catches.

"So . . . . What's your name?" Said the Captain.

I thought fast . . . I don't want to use my real name . . . .

"Jonah . . . . Jonah Smith!"

I smiled and shook his hand.

"Well Jonah, We will be back at Riviera Beach in about an hour. You are one . . . lucky son of a bitch!"

He was carefully checking his radar, "So . . . I guess the whale spit you out . . . . huh?"

"Something like that!" I said.

Bennington Blue Water Charters put me off on the dock. I thanked him and walked away from the marina and into a shipyard a few blocks up the road. I was looking for a place to sleep for the evening. I had no money or ID . . . *and no computer.* Next to the shipyard was a small sea freight company that had containers all over. I found a container that was unlocked, opened the end, and climbed inside. I moved around some pallets and cardboard and created a nest for the evening.

They were moving other containers around me with a giant forklift and I had to watch carefully to be sure I didn't get moved too.

During the evening, after everyone had gone home, I walked around the yard and watched some people in a big rusty grey freighter. It was tied to the sea wall, along with a few other vessels.

I stood beside a container as I heard screaming from the cabin. Through the glass of the cabin, I could see a dark haired woman that was being beaten by her drunken husband. He beat her repeatedly as she finally fell to the floor. He then pulled a gun on her, put it against her head and pulled the trigger. I waited for the "BANG". *Nothing?* I considered walking away from this situation. I don't need another problem, but no one deserves to be treated like he was treating her

"*CLICK*". Her husband thought that this was hilarious, as she cried and shook in fear at his feet. He kicked her until she no longer responded.

That's enough ... I can't allow that to continue. I moved closer to the seawall.

He left the ship and had the yardman drive him off of the property. I walked slowly and carefully toward the freighter. I didn't know if that one man was the only crew on the ship.

I crept up the gangplank and onto the deck as the huge dock lines squeaked and moaned. I slowly opened the steel door and found myself in a stairway landing. I went up, and as my head got to the floor level, I could see her lying in the floor. Her head was bleeding and her dark brown hair was in the blood on the floor. She was bare footed with a lacy white dress that was also spotted with blood, and dust from the floor. I walked toward her as I watched all around to be sure that she was alone. I moved to her face and moved her head to see if she was alive.

"DON'T HURT ME! DON'T HURT ME!" as she scooted across the floor and backed herself into the corner.

"It's okay! I'm here to help!"

She allowed me to get closer.

"Can you stand up?" I asked.

She stood slowly using the corner to stabilize herself. I put my arm around her as she lost her balance and grabbed me. I helped her over to a couch and sat her down while I found a towel. I cleaned the blood from her face and hair. She looked Hispanic with dark eyes and dark hair. Her nails were painted and she wore a chain around her neck with a cross on it. She didn't look like she belonged here.

"Let me help you get away from your husband before he gets back."

She was starting to make more sense and wanted to get some things from the master cabin. I followed her to a flight bag that lay against the wall. She loaded the bag with a few changes of clothes, shoes, and makeup. She went to the other side of the bed and got a gun from the drawer, and a briefcase from under the bed. She went into the bathroom without closing the door and took her dress off right in front of me. She ran the water and quickly washed her body in front of the sink. Her breasts were firm and she had no need for a bra. I stood watching her, until she pushed the bathroom door closed. This entire time in the cabin lasted about five minutes. She was in a big hurry and so was I.

While she finished changing clothes, I saw some money lying on the dresser. I picked up the pile and flipped through it. I pulled a one hundred and a few twenties from the middle and put the rest of it back. I found some clothes in the closet that would fit me and rolled them up for later.

She came running from the bathroom and had covered up most of her facial damage with makeup. She had a scarf over her hair. She wore a pair of Levi's and a dark blue Costa Rica T-shirt with a tree frog on it.

I looked down at her black high heels. "It will be hard to run in those!"

"I'm not running!"

She stopped, looking at herself in the mirror, and picked up some car keys from the dresser.

"Are you staying?" She said as she walked out the door.

We ran off of the freighter and she led me to a new, black, BMW. I jumped into the passenger side, and we were off of the property. She drove like a crazy woman but as much as she worried me, she seemed to have the reflexes for it. We got through town and she hit I-95 south and blended into the traffic.

It was 2AM . . . . here in the Twilight Zone.

"What is your name?" I asked . . . "I am Jonah . . . Jonah Smith!"

"My name is Lisa." She jerked into the next lane and passed a truck.

"Well . . . Lisa . . . . I think we better get off the interstate, and find a hotel so I can patch up your head. You are still bleeding."

She reached up and touched her head and saw that I was right.

"Do you know where you are going?" I asked.

"No. I just have to get away." She admitted.

"Get off up here . . . onto 441-W."

* * *

We paid cash for gas and a hotel in Belle Glade at the bottom of Lake Okeechobee. She laid on the bed as I worked on getting a butterfly to hold her cut together.

"So how did you end up at the freighter?" She asked.

"*Hold still* . . . I overheard a drug deal and the bad guys dumped me into the ocean . . . to kill me. I was picked up by a fishing boat and brought in near where you were." I said as if it were an everyday occurrence.

"It sounds like we both have had some bad experiences."

She looked at me to see if I was serious.

She held my arm with her hands as she put her head against my shoulder and closed her eyes.

She was starting to doze off and slipped further under her covers.

We were both exhausted. I turned out the light at 4AM. She slept in her bed, and I moved over to mine

*   *   *

I was awakened by people leaving the hotel, and I was starving. Lisa was out cold, so I kept the room dark and walked over to Waffle House. I bought two breakfasts to go. As we sat on her bed with her still holding the sheets against her body, we ate our first meal together. It was the first time I saw her smile.

I turned on the TV and scanned for news that covered the Palm Beach area. There was nothing that concerned us. We leaned against the headboard and finished our coffee.

She smiled at me again, and I turned off the TV.

"What?" as I smiled back at her.

"Next time . . . . I like amaretto in my coffee! Lots of amaretto! Just think of it as *amaretto with coffee*,"

She continued smiling and handed me her empty cup.

Chapter 2

Lisa still looked very beat up, as she changed into a light green summer dress. I drove toward I-75 with the sunroof retracted on her BMW, the wind had blown the dress up to the top of her legs and I could clearly see the injuries on her body from the kicking. She had pulled a pillow from the back seat, rested her head against the window, and had been asleep for the last hour. I took Rt.80 as far as Fort Myers, and headed North on I-75. As I passed the Samoset exit I started looking for I-275W which is a quick route to my favorite yacht broker over in St. Petersburg.

"Lisa .... Wake up!!! We're about to cross the Howard Franklin Bridge. It's the biggest bridge I've ever been on." She sat up straight in the seat and gazed out of the window.

"So Jonah ... where are you taking me?"

"I have a friend over here that is a yacht broker. He will find us a comfortable yacht that's not going to be shown for a while and let us hide out on it until we feel safe." I said.

* * *

"Mr. Monelle! How are you doing?" I said.

"Mr. *Bradford*! Long time! What can I do for you?" as we shook hands.

Lisa looked at me questioning the name.

"Later!" I whispered.

"This is my new friend Lisa."

He checked out her bruises and looked at me.

"Come into my office."

His look became serious and he closed the door.

"So Jonah! ... Are you two in trouble?" Asked James.

"Not any more. We just need some cooling off time. Do you have anything that we can occupy for a couple weeks?"

"First tell me the story! I can't get involved in anything that could hurt the business." He said, with a look of hesitation in his eyes.

"I understand!"

Lisa and I took turns explaining all the events that led up to our appearance in Jim's office.

Jim had his chair leaned back against the wall and had been studying our body language while we talked. The office became uncomfortably quite while he just sat looking back and forth at us.

"Sounds like you are both lucky to be alive!"

He started leafing through his brokerage papers.

"HERE! I just got this one in. It's from an estate, so nothing will be happening on it until after it is all settled. It's exactly as I got it. It hasn't been cleaned, checked, or anything. I know that you are qualified to take care of that for me! Does it sound like a deal?"

"What is it?" I asked.

He slid the papers across the desk as I studied.

Tayana 48' CC 1997 Estimated sale price $375,000.

"I'm going to list it for $390,000 and see if there's any interest. I don't get one of these very often!" Said Jim.

"Sounds like we have a deal!"

I glanced at Lisa and she was shaking her head . . . *yes.*

Jim gave us the key and the dock location. He turned off the lights, locked the doors, and went home for the night. It was great to have a friend that trusted me like this.

I looked at the papers while we walked down the dock. It was beautiful. All of the teak was covered in black canvas as was the bimini and dodger. The port lights were all stainless steel and I could see the high quality fittings even from here. I felt dizzy as I stared up the mast. When I looked down, Lisa was already on the boat waiting by the companionway door. We unlocked the hatch and went below. We both froze in place, admiring the open space. I was not sure how I could ever go back to my boat.

While I admired all of the solid . . . teak interior, Lisa found sheets to put on the bed in the huge master cabin. The front cabin was buried in sail bags, cockpit cushions, life preservers, and water toys.

"We'll get into that tomorrow." I said.

I found the shore power cord, plugged it in, and then turned on the fridge and air conditioning. When I turned and looked for Lisa she was asleep on the bed. It felt good to see her that secure and relaxed. I turned out the light in the cabin and pulled the hatch closed. The air conditioner hummed and made the temperature bearable in the boat. I played with the digital TV until my stomach growled for sustenance. I quietly left the boat and went in search of food.

The marina bar had already closed, but the owner told me that he had eggs and enough things in the back to make a couple omelets. He continued running his daily totals, allowing me time to cook. I thanked him, walked to the back and started cracking eggs.

* * *

"Oh!! These are sooo good!" Said Lisa.

"I cook them in butter and top them off with cream cheese." I ate my last bite.

She laid her head on my lap as I finished my Dr. Pepper and reclined against the headboard. Her eyes closed again as I picked through her hair checking the cut. It was healing well.

"It's looking pretty good. You should be able to wash your hair tomorrow! How did it get cut anyway?"

"After Raymond got done punching on me, he hit me broadside with the pistol"

"Why was he so mad anyway?" I asked.

She turned onto her back and looked straight up at me.

"I was kidnapped from Costa Rica. He owns a freighter business. It is only a small freighter business, but he thinks he's soooo important! One day while my sister and I were hitchhiking to our jobs, Raymond and some of his men picked up the two of us from the bus intersection. My sister got out at the Avis Car Rental . . . *where she works* . . . and I rode on into town. He turned before we got to my job and he drove toward the docks. When we got to the docks, the boat was ready to leave. Raymond's men drug me aboard and locked me in a cabin with other people. The night that you helped me is the first time that I have been off his boat since that day." She said quietly.

"Does he beat you like this often?"

"Only when he gets drunk . . . this is a few times a week. He raped me when we were coming across the Gulf, and I almost killed him with a riggers pin. Now he is afraid to rape me and just likes to beat me and scream at me. He's probably glad that I'm gone!"

She went deep into her thoughts.

I just sat and processed all of what she said.

I mentally reviewed her story and tried to visualize the abuse and degradation she endured to survive an ocean crossing in captivity.

"He needs to be dealt with!" My blood pressure was rising as I remembered the brief case.

"What's in the brief case?" I asked.

She got off of the bed, and left the cabin. She returned with the briefcase and a sinister smile. She climbed back up next to me, and lay against the pillows. She pulled the heavy briefcase onto her lap. After dialing in the combination, the case was opened.

It was full of American Currency and a small group of Costa Rican Colones. The Colones were red and said 1000 each. I picked some up and inspected them.

"Don't be impressed. A 1000 Colone is worth about a $1.98. If you go into a Burger King in my country a #2-value meal will cost you $3,027 Colones. You should see the gas pumps when you fill up." as she giggled.

"So how much money is in here?" I asked.

"Approximately $900,000 *North American*." She said calmly.

"Why do you have that much in a brief case?" I asked.

"I don't . . . . Raymond . . . DID! Ha . . . Ha . . . Ha!"

"He was always hauling something for cash. Most of the time it was drugs, but sometimes people, too. He brought people into America illegally, and sometimes he sells people . . . ."

She went silent for a moment.

"That's probably what he had planned for me!" as she looked in my eyes.

I threw three Colones onto her lap. "There . . . is that enough?" I joked.

"That's not funny!"

And she turned her back to me.

"I'm sorry!" I said, as she smiled back over her shoulder "You're forgiven."

She smiled and put the brief case in the floor.

We walked up to the showers while the rest of the marina slept. Lisa went ahead and gently washed her hair. She carefully managed to not break open her cut. I was amazed at how shiny her hair was with nothing but cheap shampoo. She wore shorts and a long t-shirt and walked bare foot back to the boat.

Her hair was straight and hung down over her shoulders. I just wore baggy shorts, a T-shirt and my flip-flops. I was back to the boat before Lisa, and she looked beautiful as she climbed down the companionway stairs. She still had visible bruises but in general there was nothing real noticeable.

During the evening, I rolled back and forth in the bed. It takes me a while to get used to a new bed, and I think having her next to me was not helping either. On my last revolution, I stretched my arm across Lisa's chest and it ended up between her breasts. She grabbed my hand and pulled it up to her face as she laid her cheek on it and scooted tighter against me. I heard her breathing increase before we both finally went to sleep.

I woke up in the morning before her, with an erection pressed against her buns. I gently got up before she noticed and went up on deck. I went over to the bar and got two large coffees ... *one with Amaretto* .... and two fresh Cinnabon style pastries that were still hot. I took them back to the boat and served breakfast in bed.

"You are going to spoil me Mr. *Smith*" as she smiled about my alias.

"Oh yes ...." I reached out to shake her hand ...

"Good morning Lisa ... I am Jonah Bradford."

"Good to meet you Mr. Bradford ... I am Lisa Saborio!"

She tore off another tiny piece of the Cinnabon.

After breakfast we put on our working clothes and started cleaning the boat. We started on the deck and rigging with little brass wire brushes and some *Painless Stainless* polish. When the temperature neared 90 deg. we worked below deck with the air conditioner on full blast.

This boat came from an estate here in Florida, and the previous owner left the boat in the same way he left the world ... *not ready to go!* We found all sorts of personal items. Most of them we just kept putting in the trash, but occasionally we found something good. I found the boat kitty under the mattress. He left five, hundred dollar bills, and I just put them in my money clip.

"No sense in telling Monelle about that." I thought.

Lisa found a bunch of photos and started a box of items she wanted to send to his family.

"These things will be very important to his kids!" She explained.

"Yeah! Unless this woman he's got his arms around is not his wife?"

I threw it into her box.

"You are so ... *Negative!*" She said.

"*Real!*" I responded.

17

Lisa was a very hard worker. She was wearing me out trying to keep up with her. When it became time for lunch, I realized we had not bought groceries.

"Lisa ... break time ... let's go into Tampa and do some shopping!"

"I never say NO to shopping, especially when Raymond is doing all the buying!" She giggled.

She threw her rags into the sink and headed for the master cabin. She pulled her T-shirt off, dropped her shorts, and bent over to get her bag from the floor. I admired her tight buns and bare back.

She turned to see me drooling at her body, smiled, and closed the door. She came out in a pair of white slacks, a flowery blouse and white heels. She went into the head to take down her hair. I went into the cabin and put on a pair of pants that I stole from Raymond. They were a bit loose but the length was good. I put on a dress shirt and rolled up the sleeves.

"We will do the groceries last, so they stay cold." Said Lisa.

"Good idea! We both need clothes, and do you think Raymond would like to buy me a laptop computer?" I asked.

"Ohhh! Raymond loves buying laptop computers!" She said with that sinister smile and we ran up the dock.

We jumped into the BMW and sped toward Tampa. We got on I-275N and were in Tampa in 30 minutes.

Lisa liked dresses! She liked looking sexy! I had no complaint, but she was attracting attention that made me uncomfortable. I bought Levi's, a few more pairs of shorts, and a bunch of light weight sport shirts. After a new pair of tennis shoes, I was ready to hunt for the laptop.

To a writer, typing is like a drug addiction. Lisa was not ready to stop yet, so I asked the store manager for a good local computer store. He gave me directions to a Best Buy three blocks away, and I told Lisa where to find me.

I bought a new laptop with a super fast processor and a huge hard drive. I added a carry case and a 1TB, external hard drive. I could back up the entire computer and it would fit in my pocket.

It was already loaded with Windows and MS Office Ultimate. I was a happy boy as I walked back to the clothing shop. The storeowner caught me when I came into the shop and told me that she went to another shop on the corner. I went over there, and she was checking out with a bag in each arm. We walked back to the car, and then went searching for a grocery.

"Lisa . . . If you were kidnapped from Costa Rica . . . whose car is this?"

"Raymond's! He has three." She said nonchalantly.

"Uhh Huhh! And do you have a passport?" I carefully asked.

"Yes! In my top drawer of my dresser in Limon!"

"Limon . . . as in Costa Rica?" I questioned.

"Yes! I didn't take my passport to work with me!"

She was making me nervous. *Stolen money . . . stolen car . . . illegal alien . . . beaten and raped . . .*

"Lisa . . . Let's just get a few groceries. I think we need to go back to the east coast and spend some time at my house. We have a lot of things we need to get worked out."

She looked at me concerned, and shook her head.

We loaded the dock cart and stocked the boat for the next week. Lisa modeled her purchases for me over the next hour and I was amazed at how well she cleans up. During clothes changes, I was setting up the Wi-Fi connection on the new computer. *"I can't help it! I am a writer!"*

The show was almost over, and for the grand finale, she modeled a black corset, black lacy panties with a garter, and thigh high French silk hose. When she slipped on her black heels, I was done.

I shut the screen on the laptop and stood. She slowly danced toward me with a serious smile. I could detect an underlying emotion of fear . . . *of me* . . . and the need for my approval. She continued dancing as she pushed her body against mine and rubbed her breasts against my chest. She looked up at me with her big brown eyes. I kissed her, and placed my hands on her hips as I backed her toward the Master Cabin.

Chapter 3

Over the next few days we finished detailing the boat and turned it back over to Jim. I thanked him once again as he admired the beautiful woman holding my hand.

"Come back and detail my inventory . . . ANY time!"

He waved to us walking away.

We drove on I-75 toward Orlando and hit the Rt.528 Toll Rd. back over to I-95. The trip took the entire day as we lost time on the Rt.4 bypass from a semi-truck wreck in the curve. I was glad to see my house, with the mailbox full of bills, and the porch light still on.

"It's not much, but this is it!" We got out of the car and got our bags from the trunk. I was glad that I had cleaned it up recently. There were no dirty clothes piled in the bathroom. They were all in the drier. We left the bags in the dining room and went directly to my walk in shower.

About the time I had shampoo lather on my head, Lisa came scooting in beside me telling me that I take too long. I squirted her with the shampoo and that was the beginning of the war. She put her hand on the showerhead and shot it into my face. I spread cream rinse all over her breasts as she tried to get the shampoo out of her eyes. She stood under the showerhead to rinse. I vacated the shower, reached in and turned off the *hot* water.

"AAAAHHH!!! You're dead!!"

She finished rinsing her hair, wrapped a towel around her head, and chased me into the living room completely naked. All the lights were out in the living room. I grabbed her and pressed her wet body up against the sliding glass doors. I reached down below her belly button with my right hand. *The battle was over,* with her back against the glass and her legs wrapped around my waist.

We slept in my big king size bed and woke up in the morning with the Mocking Birds singing for my return. They like to build nests in my Jasmine bushes since they all know that I will prune around them until their eggs hatch.

My grass was *goat* height, but overall it wasn't that bad. We sat at the dining room table and discussed what to do next. We drank our coffee, and counted the rest of Raymond's money.

"I think we better go over to the marina and check on my boat. I'm hoping that the drug dealers have moved on and still think I'm dead. If they see me I may *really* be dead!"

"And . . . . we need to get you a passport!" I added.

I called my friend in customs and he filled out a request for *replacement* of a lost passport from Costa Rica.

"Just burn the old one when you get back and this one will have all the same numbers and everything. Here is a temporary one that I stamped for your entrance into the country dated a week ago. He got fingerprints, and made copies of her Costa Rica Driver's License and any other documentation she had in her purse. We stayed at my house for the next three weeks, and as he said, the passport was delivered to my front door.

"Doug told me he expedited it!" I said, as she showed the Fed-X man her I.D. and signed the form.

She tore open the envelope and looked at her photo and information.

"You're legal!" I commented.

"Now! Let's get the BMW out of the garage and get rid of it. You drive it and follow me, and do exactly what I do. No hot-roding! Understand?" I said sternly, and then smiled at her.

"Yes Sir . . . Master . . . Boss!"

"Smart ass!" I said.

We detailed the car for fingerprints and anything else we may have left in it. We cleaned the trunk and even the engine compartment. I got some clear rubber gloves from my painting supplies for the boat and told her to keep these on until we ditch the car. We drove the car down Rt.1 during rush hour traffic, and turned west into Melbourne. We drove across, toward I-95, pulled it into a low-income subdivision. We parked the BMW on a side road with the other cars parked on the street. I walked up to the car as she got out.

Leave the driver's window down and leave the keys in the ignition. I took the keys from her hand and wiped them off with a cotton rag. I pushed them back in the ignition and I wiped the door handle before walking back to my truck. We drove up to Bob Evans, had lunch, and drove back past were we had parked the car. The car was long gone.

"A car like that in this neighborhood will be completely stripped in another hour!"

I laughed.

"I really liked that car." Whined Lisa.

"Yeah! So did I. But not enough to die or go to prison for it!"

We drove north on Rt.1 for the next hour and pulled back into my driveway. I got a Heineken from the fridge and we sat down and watched a movie on Netflix. I sat with my hand on her leg while she cried about *a big dog that waited for its Master to come back on the train for years, after he was dead.*

The next morning Lisa suddenly missed her family.

"Can I call my sister, from your phone?" She asked.

"Sure! But all I have is a cell phone. Try to keep it as short as you can so my bill doesn't kill me." and I handed her my phone.

She started punching numbers while I went out to water my plants.

"Jonah ... Jonah ... I need to go home!" Said Lisa.

"What's up?" I asked.

"Raymond has been calling my sister. He has threatened her. If she doesn't give me up he will kill her. He is in Costa Rica right now!" She said almost hysterically.

"Will Raymond really do that?" I asked.

"Oh Yeah! All he needs to do is get drunk first."

I could hear the fear in her voice.

I stood and thought for a few minutes.

"Okay . . . pack! It's time for us to go to Costa Rica!" We walked to my bedroom.

I booked our tickets out of Orlando. We took my Jeep Cherokee and headed west on Rt.528.

I put the car in an off-site long-term parking lot and the shuttle took us to the USAir check in. We almost missed our flight explaining about Lisa's temporary passport, but when I mentioned Doug's name, they called and held the flight for us.

They had cell phones in the back of the seats, and after we were airborne, Lisa wanted to call her sister. There was no answer on her phone so she typed in the number for her Mother

"Hello! Lisa! Where are you? That man came and got Loren, and he took her to his boat. She did not know where you were and he did not believe her. We all thought you were dead!"

"Almost momma! I . . . and a good North American friend, are coming to help. We will be there later tonight if all goes as planned . . . . I love you momma!" Lisa said with sadness.

"I love you too Lisa . . . be careful!" She said

Lisa told me about what her Mom had told her and I carefully explained that by now her sister may be beaten, raped, or possibly dead. After not getting any information from Loren, he would probably go back to her mother and start on her. Now . . . her mother knows that we are in route.

"Don't worry. We will find her . . . together."

I squeezed her hand and displayed a convincing smile.

I had put $3000 American in my laptop case and figured that would be enough in Costa Rica to buy some help. The plane sat down outside of Limon. Lisa's mother lived in the small Village outside of Estrada. We rented a car with my American Express.

I let Lisa drive since I had no idea where I was and she was the master of dodging potholes.

We checked in at Lisa's mother's home. It was a small wooden home with three small bedrooms, one bath, kitchen, living room, and covered front porch. The screen door was black with bare wood where everyone grabbed it. Most of the screened windows were open and a breeze stirred up dust as we parked against the front porch. A small woman greeted us at the front door. She squeezed Lisa and affectionately kissed her on the forehead. She looked over Lisa's shoulder with a worried look on her face. She wasn't interested in socializing as she released Lisa and told the story.

"They took Loren! Help Loren!" She said with tears starting from her dark eyes.

We immediately got back in the car. Loren's boyfriend was at the house with his friend and they jumped in the back seat. Lisa drove crazy again, but we were fighting for her sister's life.

"Raymond always docks his ship in Moin. It's on this side of Limon!" Said Lisa.

"Just go to the pier. We'll be sure he's there and then figure out our attack plan." I said.

She turned off of route 16 as the dust blew up behind us. She turned and drove along a canal until we saw some big unoccupied piers. She let off the gas pedal as we rolled up to the dock.

"This is it?" I asked.

"He's already gone." Said Loren's boyfriend.

"Where do you think he will go?" I asked.

"Back to Florida!" Said Lisa, "That's where he transfers all of his . . . *product*." as she looked at me with hopeless brown eyes.

I pulled out my cell phone and waited for a tower . . . . Nothing!

"Here!" Said one of the guys . . . "Use mine!" as he handed me his phone.

I pulled up the number from my phone and made a call to Florida on the other phone.

'Doug! This is Jonah ... What? ... Forget the caller ID! ... Look ... I am in Costa Rica. There's a vessel headed to Florida with human Cargo. Yeah! ... No ... They were kidnapped from Limon, Costa Rica. One of the hostages is Lisa's sister. Can you call Miami Coast Guard and have them intercepted? The name of the vessel ... Wait!"

"Lisa ... What's the vessel name?"

"Tom ... Tom .... Something .... UNCLE TOM!" She said.

"Doug! It's a midsize freighter called **Uncle Tom** .... Yeah ... I know!"

"Thanks Doug! Call back on this number if you need anything else."

I handed his phone back, and we all went back to Mrs. Saborio's house. The guys went home and Lisa and I spent the night with her mother. I had to sleep in her sister's room and Lisa slept in her room. Her mother monitored every sound in the house.

*   *   *

The next morning I woke up to the smell of coffee and amaretto, along with bacon, biscuits and gravy. They put the Amaretto in the coffee water while they brew it here. That is why Lisa is so addicted to it! I had finished my food and was into my third cup of coffee.

A car sped down the road and stopped next to our rental car.

"BOOM! BOOM! BOOM!! BOOM! BOOM!" At the front door.

The guys were excited and carrying on in Spanish. Loren's boyfriend burst through the unlocked door, came to the kitchen table, and crammed his cell phone against my head.

"Hello! Yes this is Jonah Bradford ... GREAT! Thanks for calling!"

"Wrong number." I said.

The screaming came from all directions in two languages as I started laughing.

"Loren's alive . . . . she's a little beat up . . . . but she's okay!

Everyone started hugging each other. Lisa repeated it in Spanish for Andrea's friend. Andreas slapped me on the back and gratefully shook my hand.

"She will be detained in Miami with eight other girls for a few days and then they will all be flown home! They are not *all* Costa Ricans!" I said, "Two were North American tourists!"

Lisa wanted me to stay until Loren got back, and knowing that we had a few days to blow, she volunteered to show me Costa Rica. I had been on the west coast before, but I had never been inland or to the east coast. One time I spent a few nights in Nautia, Mexico, on this coast, but a big thunderstorm sort of shortened my visit.

We left the house Saturday morning. We drove in moderate traffic for three hours. On the way, I saw the majority of people using the bus system or hitch hiking. Unlike the US, hitch hiking was still safe here; at least that's what the locals tell me. As a matter of fact, if you did NOT pick up people standing on corners you occasionally got a hand gesture expressing their opinion of your anti-social attitude.

Lisa picked people up regularly and even knew a few of them. It became interesting exchanging stories with the locals. Everyone was interested in North America. Most of the shops and towns that I saw were just a notch above poverty. There were city centers and some shops that were current to U.S. standards but they were scarce.

We arrived at the La Paz Water Falls before noon, and walked through the gardens and nature trails to the waterfalls. They had areas of butterflies, snakes, birds, flowers, and a nearby hotel called the Peace Lodge that offered a fireplace and Jacuzzi in every room, *if* you were rich enough to afford it.

Overall I was not that impressed with the tourist attractions. I usually am not! What I *was* impressed with were the people that survive here. Some of the people we picked up on the way back, hitch hiked for an hour to work an eight hour job, only to get off work and hitch for an hour to go home .... every day! Most of them had a small home or apartment, a few kids, and couldn't even afford a car.

On the way back she showed me some beaches that were great for surfers. One beach she told me was very private and you had to climb down a seventy-foot long rope ladder to get to it. Usually surfers that go there take a tent and spend several days.

Sunday we all went to church. It was very casual, and I wish I could have got a camera inside. The architecture of the church must have been hundreds of years old. The sides were built from cut stone as were the floors and steps. The windows were pointed and tall with the leaded glass set back into the eighteen inch thick walls. The seating was made from a wood that resembled cherry and had a cherub carved in both ends of each section. Big stone columns supported overhead beams that supported an intricately carved truss system that I looked at more than the minister.

Afterwards there was a festival in Limon. There was a parade, and a lot of the shops were open just for the festival. The festival was very loud and the women were very scantily dressed. When I started rating all the girls on the floats .... *from 1 to 10* .... Lisa decided that it was time to go shopping.

At one point I saw a bunch of men with weapons and military uniforms. Lisa advised me not to look at them.

"They are from Panama. Drug traffickers! We are just an hour from Panama!" She said and pulled me into a tourist, clothing shop. I squeezed around a few tourists while Lisa looked at the latest styles in the front of the store.

"She bought more sexy dresses and another pair of heels while I bought a shirt that said *Costa Rica*, on it. I bought my maximum amount of coffee that I could take home without paying duties, and we headed back to the house.

* * *

I could smell the food coming through the front screen door even before we entered the house. Momma Saborio, had supper on the stove and we were starving. I peeked into the pan and found beef chunks marinating slowly in brown gravy. In a pan steaming in the sink was a colander of noodles. We had shopped right through lunch and I was feeling it now. I sampled the beef with a fork. She started yelling at me in Spanish, and beating my back with a dishtowel. I laughed and ran for the living room.

After super I sat on the couch and watched the Jefferson's in Spanish on the TV. Lisa sat in the floor between my legs, leaning against the couch. I massaged her shoulders as she played with my legs. Momma Saborio spent more time giving us both dirty looks, then watching TV. We grabbed a passionate kiss in the hallway before going to our separate bedrooms for the night . . . . AAAahhh!

Monday morning, before sunrise, Lisa snuck into my bedroom. She woke me up with a kiss and I ran my hand up under her dress.

"Noooo!" She whispered, "I have to go to work. I will be home about 6:00."

I grabbed her and pulled her onto the bed. She pounded on me and wiggled her way to freedom. With a big horney smile on her face she wiggled her finger at me and pulled the door shut. I heard the car start and disappear down the road. I slept a bit longer until I heard Momma Saborio cooking breakfast. I got up and went into the kitchen. She handed me some toast and butter and motioned for me to help. I got to work and in a few minutes she was making jokes about me that I didn't understand, and laughing. I think she thought that I may be a resident son in law in the learning stages. Loren's boyfriend showed up in time to eat with us, and then he took Momma into town for . . . *something?*

I did the dishes after they left and went back into my bedroom. I closed the blinds on the window, and went back to bed. I was awakened by the sound of a car coming up the dirt road. It stopped in front of the house and then it left again. I lay in bed listening as someone entered the house. *The door did not even have a lock on it!* I heard the door shut and footsteps walking around on the wood floors. They came down the hallway, the doorknob turned, and Lisa quietly came into the room. She looked at herself in the full-length mirror on the back of the door. She unzipped her dress and placed it on the dresser. She stepped out of her heels and slowly slipped off her stockings. She walked back over to the mirror. I slipped out of the bed and quietly came from behind her. I grasped her hands and raised them over her head, against the door, as I pushed my body against her back. She screamed and squirmed. I held her solid. I let her turn to see me and kissed her on the lips.

"I am so horney!" I said, as I released her hands and grabbed her hips.

"She raised her knee and flattened my balls. I fell onto the bed trying to breathe.

"WHO ARE YOU? AND WHY ARE YOU IN MY BEDROOM?" She asked. Her eyes flashed with anger.

I was totally confused.

"LISA! Have you lost your mind?" I said still trying to catch my breath.

She stood looking at me with a blank look on her face.

She slowly formed a familiar sinister smile, and sat on the edge of the bed.

"I am not Lisa . . . . I am Loren! Lisa and I are *twins!*" She giggled and quickly put her dress back on.

I rolled off of the bed in my boxer shorts as *LOREN* . . . . went into the kitchen.

I jumped from the bed and caught up with her, standing by the sink.

"LOREN . . . GOOD TO MEET YOU! I am Jonah Bradford. I called in the Coast Guard rescue for you!" as I rubbed my balls.

"Sorry about that!" She smiled at me, and glanced down at my boxer shorts, "but after what I have been through, you are lucky that I didn't stab you."

"I totally understand! All is forgiven!"

I poured two cups for coffee.

We sat for the rest of the morning and connected all the dots of the story. She had been mildly beaten but there were other girls that got it worse.

"The Captain was keeping me in better shape than the others, to use me as trade for some money . . . *that he said Lisa stole?*" She took a long pause.

"He kept me in the cabin with the two North American girls."

"Well . . . Jonah . . . I thank you very much for our rescue, but I am exhausted. I want to get a shower and go to bed."

My eyebrows must have gone up!

"*BY MYSELF* . . . in my bed!

As of now you are officially evicted!" She said with a smile.

I stuck out my bottom lip as she stood and headed for the *banyo.*

I listened to her in the shower. When she came out of the bathroom and walked to the refrigerator in a towel, I could see a duplicate Lisa. The only giveaway is how they do their hair.

She wiggled her hips when she strutted past me, and went into my . . . *her* . . . room and closed the door.

The door opened a few inches. I stood and walked toward it. As I got closer it opened a bit wider. Her hand came from inside with my clothes in it. I took the clothes, and the door shut as I stood there holding them.

The door slowly opened again and this time . . . she handed me her damp towel.

"You are soooo bad!" I said . . . as I heard her giggling through the door!

Chapter 4

Momma Saborio was dropped off in time for lunch. Loren's boyfriend was starting to drive away. I ran across the kitchen, through the screen door, and stopped him. I told him Loren was in the house and he jumped from the car, ran through the kitchen, and pounded on her door. I went over, turned his car off, and closed his door.

It was rough watching them kiss and hug. I felt betrayed by Lisa?

Momma and I went out on the front porch and gave them some quality time to *talk*. There wasn't *anything else* going to happen in *Momma's house!*

I called Lisa and she came home early. Everyone for a mile around was at the house and Lisa and I took that as an opportunity to reduce some stress. We walked down a long trail that led to an unused canal which ran parallel to the ocean.

We found some soft grass with an abandoned old wooden boat on one side. There were tall weeds on the other side and the clothes came off in a frenzy.

Afterwards, we lie there looking at the setting sun and the birds diving on the water.

"Come back to America with me." I whispered.

She looked into my eyes for a long time and I saw them filling with tears . . . I knew I had my answer.

"Why not?" I asked.

"My family is here. I grew up here! I have a job here!" She said.

"Do you have a lover here?" I asked.

"At the moment ... yes!" She smiled ... "You stay here!"

"I've already thought about it. Costa Rica is not for me. I'm used to I-95 and Mickey Mouse. If my windows don't rattle from a Rocket Launch, my life is not complete. I love you Lisa, but I have to go back to North America."

She hugged me and nothing else was said. We walked back to the house and I think Momma Saborio's mental powers picked up on us immediately. Even though her missing daughter had returned, she remained sad and went to bed early.

I slept on the couch, and in the morning I packed my bags before anyone got up.

Momma hugged me at the front door and told me she would miss me ... in English! I got in the car with Lisa and she took me to the airport. Lisa leaned across the seat and kissed me. I stepped out of the car and got my luggage from the back. I reached in the window and put my hand against her soft face before I turned and walked into the airport.

*   *   *

I got off of the plane at Orlando International, went downstairs, and got my luggage off of the conveyer belt. I took the shuttle to the long term parking lot and paid the bill for my Jeep as they brought it up to the office. It was only forty-five minutes to my house from here, and I was anxious to get home. I still had a little over a half tank of gas and I sat the cruise control on 77mph.

After living with the Saborios, my house seemed so empty. I walked around my yard, and up and down my hallway. Finally, after putting away my clothes, I grabbed my laptop case and headed for the boat.

*   *   *

I stood beside my truck and looked at the marina. The Nordhaven was gone and I proceeded down my dock and opened up the boat. I turned the air conditioner down, opened a cold beer from the cooler, and walked around the other docks checking for trouble and visiting my friends.

It felt good to be back on the water. The trip ended back at my boat. The cabin had chilled down, I cracked open another Heineken, and took it up into the cockpit. I leaned against the cabin and pulled the laptop out of the case. I usually slide the laptop into a separate padded pouch that fits snugly inside the computer case. Today . . . the laptop was sitting on top of the pouch.

"I guess I was in a hurry?" I said aloud.

I moved the pad and below it was an envelope. I opened it and found a card from Lisa.

"I will always treasure our time together." Love Lisa

I came here with the intention of starting a new book and using a lot of my Costa Rican experiences to help. Right now my brain was so fried that I just closed up the boat and went back home.

* * *

I laid the computer on the table and sat in the leather recliner. I stared at the screen of the TV that was not on. I remembered the brief case that Lisa had me lock in the safe in the hallway. I went down the hallway and opened my cell phone. I looked up a number . . . SAFE. The combination displayed on the screen like an odd phone number. I stopped at the last number and closed the phone. I turned the heavy lever and pulled the door.

I stared into the safe a long time. Finally I slammed the door shut with a solid *clank*, pushed the lever to the left, and spun the dial. I sat in the hallway staring at the safe trying to rationalize the symbolic gesture that Lisa left me.

"I guess it's over?" I said aloud.

The brief case was gone and the safe had been re-locked? She must have watched me get the combination from my phone.

I walked into my bedroom and pulled my duffle bag from under the bed. Once I decided my next direction, I was a man with a mission. It took me about five minutes to pack clothes and necessities, and another fifteen to pack two boxes of groceries. In twenty minutes, it was all in the back of my truck and I was back in route to the marina. The lights at the Coastal Railroad crossing started blinking as the gates began to descend. I jerked a last minute right into the Seven-Eleven parking lot and parked in front of the double glass doors. I bought two cases of Heineken, a bag of caramel creams, and put them in the back of the truck with the duffle bag, while I waited for the train.

It was a cool night with a full moon and I hit the power window buttons with the tips of my fingers. I felt the night air blow through the cab. I dropped to 35 miles an hour and drove through the well-lit tourist area of town. I stopped at the light as teenagers had their hands on each other laughing loudly as they crossed the street. I listened to the music playing from the bar behind the palm trees. I hit the gas suddenly when I realized that the light had turned green. It is okay. There was no one else out here tonight. I crossed into the right lane and exited into the Marina.

I parked away from the dock to allow others to park closer, and went empty handed to find a dock cart.

The boards on the dock made a ticking clock sound as I rolled the cart on its hard rubber wheels. The tide was out, so it was a long step down onto the deck. I stacked everything behind the dodger, and returned the cart to its sacred home, wedged between a post and a dock box. If it was left in the open, the wind would blow it off and someone would have to fish it out of the water tomorrow. With all provisioning stowed in its proper location and the shore power cord rolled neatly, tied, and stowed, I sat down with a cold beer. I leaned against the cabin and looked at the moons reflection across the water. I thought of Lisa and wondered if she could see this moon, in Costa Rica.

When I realized my eyes were not focusing clearly, I finished the beer and went below to get the keys for the diesel. I switched the panel over to the 12V circuits and flipped the big red switches below the sink in the head. I went back up, started the diesel, and let it idle as I went around, closed certain thru-hull valves, and untied the dock lines. I left one tied by the starboard bow and let it slide from the piling as I slowly crept past. A few people came up from their dimly lit cabins, watching me chatter past quietly wondering what kind of fool would leave the dock at 10PM with a low, but rising tide.

"*A fool with a broken heart.*" I whispered, as I waved to a man admiring my exodus.

I felt the keel drag in the channel as I left the marina. It was minor so I bumped the throttle and powered through.

"You won't read that maneuver in Chapman's." I said, looking back at the fading marina lights.

I made it south down the ICW as far as the drawbridge and anchored on the North side until morning. After watching the anchor for an hour, and drinking two more beers, I went below and slept the rest of the evening.

* * *

I woke up at 9AM. By 10AM I was idling behind a 44' ketch waiting for the locks to set us free. We both motored past Blue Point and the cruise ships, and then raised the sails together as we broke into blue water. I waved to them as he left me in his wake. I only had my main sail up so far and he had his wife and kids working like a racing crew. I admired the shape of his sails and how picturesque the ketch was against the rising sun. I unfurled my Genoa sail and relaxed against the safety rail. I looked at my chart plotter and locked in a waypoint to aid in my return. From the ocean this coast all looks very similar.

So why am I sailing? I thought to myself.

I thought about this for a while and realized that any time I had a situation that was out of my control, I have always ran to my other lover, the ocean.

I sailed slightly southeast with no particular destination in mind. I found myself following other sailboats in the distance and not even watching my navigation. I sailed through the evening, sleeping for four hours, and waking up to a cloudy day with light drizzle in the air. The Beneteau could have cared less. It was still just water, and even a day without sunshine was better to her, than a day tied to the dock.

Anticipating that a storm may follow this mild preview, I studied my charts and found my nearest landfall to be the northern end of Grand Bahamas Island. I changed the bearings on the autopilot, and went below to visit the head and close all the hatches. Sure enough . . . the rain became more intense and I stayed under the bimini hugging the wheel to stay dry. I sneezed a few times before the chill sent me below for warmer clothes. The wind increased to 25 knots with gusts that hit 30 to 35 knots. The ocean became rough and I questioned my sanity for sailing alone. I battled the weather for five more hours. I finally saw a few rays of sunlight ahead as the rain passed toward the United States.

The timing could not have been better. I saw Grand Bahamas coming into view. I checked the plotter and decided where to anchor. I sailed two more hours before I was able to drop the hook in ten foot of warm water off the coast. I threw out a second anchor and went below. I cooked a miniscule meal and a pot of coffee. I kept most of the hatches closed to contain the heat from the stove. I could not shake the chill in my bones. I ate, flipped on my anchor light, and wrapped myself in blankets in the V-berth. I got hot a few times, kicked off the blankets, only to freeze again and layer them back on as my body shuddered.

In the morning I noticed other sailboats on docks. I motored in slowly and backed the Beneteau into a slip. A young native boy with short hair and unusually white teeth helped me tie off. I handed him a five and he directed me to the office. I looked at the big blue and white sign as I tucked my passport and money into my pocket.

"*White Sands Marina*" I saw very little white sand and the ... *marina* ... was an old railroad type ramp running out of the water to a corrugated metal shed. I walked across the wooden deck and opened a squeaky wood screen door to the office.

"Good morning!" Said a beautiful young native girl with a big smile.

"Morning ... I need a slip for the day."

It required all of my effort just to stand there and act conscious.

She pushed some papers across the counter and I handed her my ship papers.

"Okay Mr. Bradford ... 35' at $1.10 per foot, is aaaaaaaaa ... $38.50 for the night. That includes 30-amp electric, water, and the shower is behind the office.

"Wow! Good deal! I handed her my credit card. She made a copy, rolled the receipt, and shoved it into a cubbyhole with my slip number below it.

"Mr. Bradford ... Are you okay?" She said looking more than a little concerned with the way I looked.

"Yeah .... I think I picked up a little cold on the crossing. Do you have any Cleriflu?" I said trying to ease her concern.

"No ... and it's a long way into town. The Queens Highway ends just past our driveway."

"Great! Thanks anyway!"

I picked up my papers and marched back to the boat. I went below, found my blankets, and went back to bed.

I was awakened with a pain in my abdomen that made me run to the head. I sat ... and kept pumping the handle beside the throne. My stomach decided to join the torture and release its content too. I sat on the throne with my head in the sink, afraid to move.

When the cramps subsided, I returned to my cabin, I felt weak, and beaten, and then I felt a chill that made my teeth chatter uncontrollably. I piled all of the blankets and a beach towel on top of me and curled into a fetal position.

"*BOOM . . . BOOM . . . BOOM . . . BOOM . . . !*"

I jumped from the V-berth and tried to remember where I was. I slid the companionway door back and raised my head above deck.

"Mr. Bradford! Are you all right?" Ask the native girl from the office.

"Not really. I have been . . . sick." Came my croaky response.

"Can I come below?" She asked.

"Sure . . . . but the cabin is a mess . . . . I warn you!"

I watched her beautiful cocoa legs step over the bottom half of the door and carefully descend the stairway. She looked at me questionably as I realized that I stood in my boxer shorts with a blanket wrapped around my body. She stood and looked around the cabin, and then put her hand on my head. Then she proceeded to push me toward the V-berth.

I was glad to go, and fell into a deep sleep. While I sleep she cleaned up the boat.

*   *   *

"Mr. Bradford . . . . JONAH!" She whispered with her soft Cruzan accent.

"Huh!" as I took the pillow off my face.

"Get up. I brought you some hot food."

She sat at the galley table with me and made sure I ate all of my soup and drank my water. She put her hand on my forehead.

"You're still burning up."

She pushed me back into the V-berth and tucked me in. I started shivering again.

She crawled into the V-berth and squeezed her body against me to help me control my shaking. Again I went back to sleep. *I just cannot seem to stay awake.* I woke up during the night, went to the head, and noticed that she had left after closing up the cabin. I returned to the warm blankets and went back to sleep.

*   *   *

"Jonah! JONAH!" Came that soft Cruzan voice again.

"Yeah! . . . Good morning!" as I rolled over in the bed.

"I brought you an island remedy. It taste terrible but this cure is very rare. It is transparent seaweed that grows in the deep ocean. Sometimes after a bad storm we can find it on the beaches if you know what to look for. I boiled it into a tea. "Here! . . Drink it straight down."

She ordered.

I did as she instructed and almost vomited from the taste. I forced the last liquid from the bottom of the cup and fell back into the bed. I stayed awake long enough to see her sit down at the galley table with a red and black book, and smile at me.

I didn't move all night and woke up in the morning with the chills gone and a scantily dressed island beauty next to me. I remembered parts of the past three days, but was missing a lot. I raised the covers and glanced below to see her body. By the time I memorized it, and photo-copied it . . . all the way to her face, she had woke up and was smiling at me.

"I see you are feeling better . . . yes?"

"Yes." My face turned red from being caught.

I turned on my side and put my hand on her hip.

"So what is your name?"

"Zuri"

"Zuri? . . . That's a first. Thank you for taking care of me. Your Voodoo Tea seems to have worked. I feel pretty good!"

I was scooting her T-shirt up a bit at a time. About the time I felt her bare hip, the shirt caught. She reached down and pulled it down, almost to her knees.

"Who is . . . *Lisa?*" She asked.

"How do you know about Lisa?"

"Last night, you pulled yourself against my hips and called me Lisa."

"Oh . . . I wish I remembered!

Lisa is my X-girlfriend. She lives in Costa Rica and I live in Florida, and neither of us wanted to move. So . . . she's my X."

"Good!" and she slowly pulled her T-shirt back up until it slid over her bare breasts and off into the floor.

Zuri spent the next week taking care of me like a mother during the day, and transforming into a lover at night. Sometimes she stayed a lover into the daylight too. She was an unusual woman with long black hair, cocoa colored skin, and light blue eyes. If she looked into my eyes, I could refuse her nothing, but lucky me . . . the things that she wanted was usually just more of me.

She drove me around the island and shared her private spots with me as we both asked questions and learned more about each other. One day she took me down an old beach trail in her little white Fiat. The brush was so thick that it scratched down the sides of her car as we drove. We came out next to the ruins of an old building that had a pool in the center of a dozen limestone arches.

"It's fed by the oceans tidal changes." She said. "That's how it stays warm and clean."

I took photos of the unique structure and when I turned around she was sliding her cut off blue jeans down her legs. She pranced around posing for me as I clicked away at her outdoor stripper act. She dove into the pool.

"OOOoohhhh . . . . It's so warm!" She said swimming to the other side.

I quickly abandoned my clothes, laid the camera on top of them, and joined her in the pool. It was a magical place. There was no roof on the arches so the sun maintained the temperature with shaded edges provided by the columns. The foreplay was in the water, but the climax was in the vanilla grass that was growing around the pool. She continued sitting on me afterwards and finally fell forward with her head on my chest. She went to sleep like that until I woke her to go home.

"I feel so safe with you." She said.

"Obviously . . . Do you know that you snore?"

"DO NOT!"

"DO TOO!" as we both broke out laughing.

"You are the only person that I have ever showed this place to." She said softly.

"It's a beautiful place . . . Thank you for sharing it with me."

I reached back and placed my hand between her legs. "And thank you, for sharing this with me." I jumped up and ran for the car with her right behind me.

We arrived back at the marina after both of us picked up supplies at a small wooden floor grocery. They had a few grocery carts, but there was not enough room in the isles to push one. Most of the locals just picked up a few items at a time.

She went back to the office as I tried to pull her toward the boat.

"NOOooooooo! I have to work!" She said.

"Okay . . . . see you at first break."

I sat on the end of the dock with a line in the water. I watched her daily routine, as I waited for a fish to want the shrimp I baited my hook with. She ran in and out all day, doing different things that required her attention. Fuel was delivered to the marina pumps, and she checked the order. Before noon, a man with cases of soda rolled new inventory into her storage closet. Later in the day two more sailboats filled the remaining two vacancies on her dock. They angered me when I heard them making racial comments about Zuri, and what they would like to do to her.

At the end of her workday, we shared a shower in the tiny apartment behind the office and went back out to the boat. I massaged her tired body while supper cooked in the oven.

"Lasagna is ready!" I announced

She sat in my robe and sampled the food.

"This is REALLY good!"

"Thank you. BUT! It was already made at the grocery. I just added a few ingredients and spices to it." I confessed.

"It was Friday night, and Zuri didn't have to work this weekend. The owner of the marina worked the busy weekends and always checked Zuri's books from the weekly transactions. Zuri was staring at me very seriously when I woke up. I just returned her stare.

"What?"

"You called me Lisa twice last night. Once while we were awake and didn't even realize it, and again last night as you dreamt." and the stare continued.

"And?"

"I think you still love Lisa." She said with sad blue eyes.

I looked down at the sheets.

She climbed out of the bed and got dressed as I watched. She came back to me and leaned down with her face inches from mine.

"Go find closure with Lisa. I DO NOT share." She kissed me softly, crossed the main cabin, and exited up the galley way steps.

"Zuri! . . . . ZURI!"

I heard her Fiat start as I peeked over the deck from the stairway. I saw her drive away and continue toward town. I paid my dock fee and cleared out of customs. I vacated my dock on Monday morning before sunrise. Zuri did not come in until eight.

The wind was steady, the waves were consistent, and this time I knew exactly where I was going. I did miss Lisa. I could not deny it. Zuri was a beautiful woman and I enjoyed being with her, but Lisa had engrained her *being* too deep into my soul for anyone else to fill in. Sailing alone, I had a lot of time to think, and discovered that making Lisa happy is an essential element for my own happiness.

"*Drizzle, Drazzle, Drozzle, Drome . . . . Time for this one to go home.*" I said as I laughed.

* * *

I woke up and turned off the autopilot. I was right on target for Cape Canaveral. I followed a Cruise Ship while the people on the rails waved. I continued down the channel as their Captain professionally planted the behemoth against the sea wall. I returned to my dock just before sunset, and two fellow sailors were standing in wait to receive my dock lines.

"Thanks guys!" They nodded their heads silently and returned to their boats.

I re-adjusted all the lines and tied off all of the halyards and sheets. My fenders now in place, I went below and gathered my things for the trip back to my *land* home. I found the photos of Zuri and tucked them into the side pocket of my computer case. I commandeered the dock cart and loaded everything in my truck. I had been gone two weeks! It seemed like two days.

My house was dark and empty. The porch light had burned out and projected a feeling of rejection, too. I threw the mail on the table and started carrying in the things from my truck. I piled it all in the dining room and decided to worry about it tomorrow.

I saw Lisa's flip-flops still lying by the coffee table. I forced my bare feet into them and walked around the house even though they were so tiny. I could still smell her perfume in the hallway bathroom. I missed her so much! Zuri gradually became a wet dream that was fading into non-reality.

"Just me! Dam it! I'm so *ALONE!*"

I drank a rum and coke, let it settle for a few minutes, and went to bed.

* * *

I went up to Bob Evans and had breakfast by myself. As I sat sipping my coffee and waiting on my food, I made a decision.

I opened my cell phone and still had the phone number in Costa Rica.

"Como sta! Bello Fashions!"

"Hello! . . . I am calling from North America. May I speak with Lisa Saborio?" I said anxiously waiting to hear Lisa voice.

"I am so sorry Miss Saborio doesn't work here anymore."

"Did she leave a phone number or contact information?" I ask.

"No sir! She just picked up her check and quit!"

"Okay . . . Thank you . . ." *Click!*

Suddenly I felt the rocks shaking loose in my brain as a story line came to life. I made some quick notes in my schedule book before my breakfast was delivered. I ate quickly and returned to the house and my computer. I started typing away and in 2 hours I had saved twenty-two pages. Over the next two days I could not stop. I would wake up at 3AM and type a few more pages. I would be driving down the road and suddenly see another page. It was coming together very fast. My writer energy was recharged.

This went on for a week, or two, until with *dishes in the sink, laundry in the bathroom floor, and a partial beard on my face,* I ran out of input.

I stood in the shower with shampoo running down my face. I just stood there letting the hot water pound on the top of my head.

"Jonaaah!" Came a soft voice from the bathroom door.

"Jonah?" Lisa reached into the shower and turned the hot water off.

"AAAaahhhh!" She ran from the bathroom laughing hysterically.

"How did you get in here?" I asked.

"The door was unlocked . . . dummy!"

She attacked me Costa Rican style.

"I'll remember to lock my door next time!" as I grabbed her and threw her on the bed.

She pulled off her outer clothes and looked at me seriously.

"I missed you soooo much." She whispered.

"I missed you too." As I climbed onto the bed.

We slept until it was dark and then I took her to *Paul's,* for a really great supper. I wore dress pants and a dress shirt while Lisa dressed in a full length black gown and heels. It was a very romantic evening with our candle lit table on the water front. We continued talking while we ate. I wanted to ask her about the money in the safe, but decided not to. We left a ten-dollar tip and headed for the house.

I so enjoy watching her take her clothes off. She moves like an art form.

"Can you unzip this for me?" I grabbed her long zipper and pulled it very . . . slowly.

* * *

We spent the next few days hanging around the house and occasionally visiting the boat.

> *Both of us had the same immediate need*
> *to hold each other tightly.*

Sometimes one of us would wake up at two or three o'clock in the morning and start it up again.

We decided that before we did anything that could resemble permanent; we should take a long vacation and get to know each other under more realistic conditions. I have always liked cruising in the Caribbean and Lisa had never been to the islands. My sailboat is a Beneteau 34 sloop. It is a good solid boat, built in France. Lisa had fun on the boat but thought that during a long vacation it may feel a little bit cramped. I knew that she was remembering the big Tayana that we stayed on over in St. Petersburg. That boat is a whole different animal compared to mine.

"Why don't we go boat shopping and see what is out there?" Said Lisa.

"Sure! How am I supposed to pay for it?" I asked.

"With the brief case silly." She laid her hand on mine.

"Where is the brief case?" I asked with a touch of suspicion in my voice.

"In a safety deposit box that I bought just before I went home. I put $400,000. in an on-line checking account, and the rest in the brief case. It's only about four or five blocks down the street!" She paused and stared at me.

"What! . . . Did you think I took it all to Costa Rica?" she said angrily.

"NOW! Do you want to go boat shopping, or do you want to keep your canoe?"

I'm always ready to go boat shopping. With so many people laid off from their jobs right now, this may be a good time to buy too. I thought.

We got out my laptop and typed in *yachtworld.com* and ran a fairly broad search description for the East Coast of Florida and the northern Caribbean. We spent the next few days printing out different boats that I liked. I had been sailing most of my life and leaned toward something that was fast, and could still bounce off of a sandbar and keep going. Lisa looked at it like an opportunity to buy a luxury waterfront condominium. We had it narrowed down to four boats.

Three of them were here in Florida. Two were on the East Coast and one was over by Fort Myers. The fourth boat was in Puerto Rico. We made a phone call to my yacht broker friend James in St. Petersburg. We let him set up the appointment for us with a local yacht broker here on *our* coast. That way, James will get a split commission for doing nothing more than making us the appointment. I like to take care of the people that take care of me.

The first vessel that we looked at was a 44' Passport in St. Augustine. It was a beautiful boat but overpriced and there was an offer on it that preceded us. The second boat was in Fort Pierce. It was a 40', center cockpit, Ketch rig. It had a beautiful interior which convinced Lisa, but it had hull scratches where it had been beat against a pier, and I really preferred a sloop, or cutter rig. We drove over to see Mr. Monelle in St. Petersburg and he showed us a 42' Cabo that looked as good as new. The name of it was the *Vacheron*.

"What in the hell does that mean?" I asked Jim.

"Hell if I know! But it's a beautiful vessel!" We all shook our heads in agreement.

"And Jonah! I still have the Tayana on the market. I can probably get that price way down for you. The heirs are anxious to settle the estate . . . but I didn't tell you that!"

"Okay! Well . . . thanks James! We're going to fly down to San Juan and look at one more sailboat down there and I'll let you know what we decide." I said.

"Well if you end up interested in that one; be sure that you get them to pay the VAT and licensing in the United States as part of your deal. The taxes on bringing one in could kill you!" He warned.

"So right! Thanks boss! . . later!!"

We got back in the car and headed for home.

We beat the traffic through Orlando and made it home just after sunset. We reviewed all of the boats that we had looked at and even searched a little further on the computer. The advertisement for the 2002 Hylas 46' in Puerto Rico still had me going but I hated to waste a trip flying down there and back for a dead end. I called the broker and he informed me that his seller was very motivated. He and his wife had had their first encounter with a big ocean storm and they left the vessel in San Juan and flew back to Texas.

"No Sir!" said the Broker, "The vessel is already registered in the United States. Its homeport is Corpus Christi." He said.

"Okay thank you! . . . Hey! If we fly down in the next day or so, would it be possible for us to spend a night or two on the boat?" I asked.

"Sure! That is a service that we do allow on our higher-end vessels." Said the broker.

We booked our flight and called the Puerto Rican broker back and he volunteered to pick us up at the airport. As soon as we saw the boat we fell in love with it but we tried not to display our excitement before we lost any price negotiations. He had relocated the boat to a dock closer to showers and restrooms and already had the shore power plugged in and the air conditioner running. There were even snacks and a bottle of wine on the galley table.

"I think we're in trouble!" I said to Lisa.

"Yes . . . I agree."

We were both ready to sign after the first 20 minutes. We tried to be critical of the vessel but after a few hours we could not find anything wrong. It felt like home to both of us, so now it was all a matter of price, and sea trials.

I loved the Master cabin with the large private head and Lisa was in love with the galley that was tight enough to be used under way and built like a custom kitchen

It was listed for $389,000, pre-owned. We made them an offer of $325,000 and waited on the vessel for a response from the owners. They came back with a counter offer of $360,000. We told the broker to call them and tell them that if they will accept $350,000 we would close the deal in the next 24 hours.

That did it, and now we were about to have a new home. We did a wire transfer from Lisa's account and did not have to touch the cash. Lisa did not want her name on the title because she felt that people connected to Captain Raymond might search her name to find her.

"That is okay with me, but how about if we name the boat the *Saborio?*" I asked.

We decided to not go home, and to sail it to Costa Rica and take her family out sailing. Lisa wanted to show off a bit, and I was having fun too.

My book was having no shortage of new input and I was typing every time the hook hit the sand. We stopped and filled all the tanks in Key West, and re-stocked the food supply. We went to a local estate auction in Marathon, and were high bidder on an original Louis Amherst painting of a bay with a sailboat and a parrot. The other bidder went out at $1400 and we hung it in the main cabin.

It was here that I realized that the deep keel was going to be a problem in the Caribbean Islands. It sailed great in the big blue water, but wrecked my nerves listening to the depth indicator beeping all the time near shore. I contacted Hylas and had them go to work on a redesign of the keel. I wanted the performance but I also wanted shallow water access. They sent the blueprints to a boatyard that is connected with the new Isla Moin Marina Development in Costa Rica. It is where their mega yacht base will be some day. I suggested this location so we could stay with Momma Saborio for a while.

Lisa thinks I am a genius!

Chapter 5

I t seems that nothing happens fast in Costa Rica, either. The keel modification drug out longer and longer. It did not seem that complicated to me and I offered to help, but it violated their insurance policy. I was so bored that I started working on boat interiors at the marina.

Once they saw the quality of my projects they tried to put me on payroll. If the government found out I was working, I would be fined and deported. I had them pay me cash, or pay Lisa, who was still a Costa Rican Citizen. They had wood here that I had never seen before. Some, I learned the hard way, could really mess you up if you inhaled the sawdust.

I found myself wishing that I had my own tools. The tools that were supplied to me were low quality, in comparison to what I was used too. I even tried to buy some and the available selection was poor. I did order a few Porter Cable tools from eBay U.S. Everyone at the marina made fun of me for being so . . . spoiled.

While they were working on the keel I had an electrician go through the bow thruster and recheck the amperage to battery balance. He added another house battery and increased the wire size to the thruster.

Lisa was bored too. She went back to Bello Fashions, and got hired to travel around to different manufacturers in Costa Rica and buy inventory for the store. Some times when she had to be gone overnight or sometimes a few days, I would go with her and we would have the opportunity to destroy a hotel room.

*It was so long between, encounters . . . that by the time we could let go, it felt similar to a **Klingon Mating Ritual.***

When business got serious with Lisa, I stayed out of the way and let her do her thing. I was not into fashion. She could spot the next trends and pinch them from the manufacturers. One day while she was beating up the company rep for a shipment of short dresses, I was out in the break room talking to the corporate vice president. He was telling me how good Lisa was and that he thought it was a shame that she did not have a business of her own.

"She could even have us produce a line of clothing custom made to her requests!" He suggested.

"What if she created a business in North America? Could you ship it to America without running up the overhead very much?" I asked.

"I think so. Let me check it out and I will call you."

I handed him my card.

Lisa came into the break room where we still sat at a plastic table.

"Okay . . . I'm good to go! She announced.

She smiled and pulled me onto my feet.

The executive stood and shook my hand.

"I'm going to go see how much money I just lost!" as he shook his head and walked away.

Lisa just giggled. We ran out the front door and headed for the hotel.

The next morning we left San Jose early, trying to beat the work traffic. We ended up in a completely stopped traffic jam, and I told her about the conversation in the break room.

"So . . . You are doing research for me too!" She said angrily.

"It just came up! He seems to think that you would be good at it, and he is checking on the cost of shipping and taxes to the

United States. I think you would be good at it, and it would be a good career move for your future!" I said.

"A career move . . . for MY FUTURE? UNHHH HUHHH! I get it!" She threw a knee up in the seat and leaned against the door. She stared at me with a serious expression on her face.

"Let's hear it! What's your plan?" She ordered.

"If you started a shop in America . . . you could sell your inventory for a lot more money. The exchange rate alone will make a big difference in itself. Let him produce your own clothing line, and you could even design it yourself."

"Oh yeah, you got it all worked out . . . don't you?" Her temper was increasing.

She opened the door and stepped out into the stopped traffic. She put her hands on the roof and leaned over looking into the car at me. Her hemline crept up as she bent over and the men in the car behind us were not complaining.

"YOU! You think you can get Lisa all set up and self-supporting, and then you don't have to feel guilty as you blow her off and run back to America!" Her anger was reaching its peak.

"LISA! It's not like that!" I injected.

"Oh yeah . . . ! Send her home to take care of momma! Dump her back in her own country and you're done with her. You had a few good months fucking the Costa Rican girl and got you a new sailboat! . . . Oh Yeah . . . time to move on now!"

Lisa had always felt . . . *third world* . . . . and I always had to be careful about things I said. She felt that I talked to her in a condescending manner when I was angry. She had no idea how much I envied and respected her.

I jumped out of the car and walked behind it smiling at the guys in the next car as I shook my head. I spun Lisa around and pushed her against the car. I put my face about 12" from hers.

"STOP! If you would just shut up and listen to me, you would see that there is a bigger picture involved here! I have no intention of leaving you here in Costa Rica. I want to help you get your business started and then we can sail all over the world getting new ideas for fashion as we go. You can email your designs back to Costa Rica and we just keep on going. We can travel, I can write my next book, and we can live happily ever after! GET IT?"

"Ever after?" as she calmed down.

Her facial expressions changed from anger to affection.

"If you'd just controlled your temper I would have told you all of this!" I said.

"Ever after?" She repeated

HONK!!!!! HONK!!!!! HONK!!!!! HONK!!!!! Saved by the horns!

She started laughing as she noticed that the traffic was moving again. She kissed me very fast and jumped back into the car. I ran around the back and the guys in the car behind us clapped for me. I jumped into the car, as my door slammed and the tires squealed.

We stopped in Siquirres and ate lunch with a room full of tourists from a bus. Lisa was smiling a lot now, and was anxious to hear the rest of my plans. I explained that I still had a lot of things to work out and most of them would be in the United States.

The roads had cleared now. We averaged about fifty miles per hour. It was my turn to drive and Lisa had gone to sleep on my lap. I knew how to get back to the house from here.

Suddenly, I felt a hand sliding up the leg of my shorts. She spent a lot of time hunting but finally found it hanging on the other side. She continued playing until I was having trouble concentrating on my driving.

"We're almost home." I said.

She pulled my pants leg back down, rubbed it through the fabric, and then moved back to her side of the car leaving me in a somewhat stressed situation. I hit my turn signal, turned left onto the dirt road to Estrada, and proceeded slowly, dodging the potholes. I parked the car in front of the house and went in the unlocked front door. I threw my flight bag on the couch while Lisa stuck her tongue out at me, went into *her* bedroom, and shut the door.

Everyone was gone, so the water was probably still hot. I pulled a change of clothes from my bag and went into the shower. I came out dressed and was still drying my hair as I looked for Lisa.

"Lisa? . . . Lisa Saborio? . . . Where are you?" I moved toward her bedroom. I slowly opened her door and peeked around the corner.

She had been sitting on the bed, looking out the window. She turned and looked at me with her hands on her breasts.

"There you are!" I smiled and moved toward her.

She backed away from me and jumped across the bed. I chased her out of her bedroom and through the house as she giggled and screamed. I caught her in the kitchen and tried to bend her over the table. She wiggled loose and ran down the hall. She was back in her bedroom and was tired of playing. She lay on her bed with a very serious look on her face.

Sex this time, was very slow and sensuous. She was thinking deeply as *she* made love to *me*.

I gladly went along with anything she wanted. There were no words, just touching and actions. It ended loudly with her jumping up and down on me and the headboard knocking against the wall. She stayed on me afterwards and stared into my eyes for a long time. I could only guess what she may have been thinking.

She looked through the open window's screen beside the bed. Her facial expression suddenly changed to a worried stare, and then to panic! She jumped from the bed and ran into the shower.

"MOMMA'S HOME!" I quickly got redressed and ran to the couch in the living room. I put my head on my pillow. I pretended to be waking up from a nap as they came through the kitchen door.

"Where's Lisa?" She asked.

"I think she's taking a shower. It has been a **hard** day."

Loren's boyfriend Andres, started snickering at my subliminal comment.

Lisa came from the bathroom about then in a robe with her hair wet.

"Hi momma!" as she went into her bedroom and shut the door. Momma went back into the kitchen and unloaded her shopping bags while Loren's boyfriend smacked me on the shoulder and smiled at me. He turned on the TV and sat down in a chair across from me.

There was a show on, totally in Spanish. What I gathered from it was that the participants could dance, or sing, and the judges rated them according to their breast size and nudity level. I am sure there had to be more to it, but that was all I got. *I was ready to go home.*

*　*　*

After supper, Lisa and I went back to the marina. It looked like they were finished with the keel. It was the shape that was on the blueprint and appeared to have several coats of bottom paint on it as it hung in the yacht lift. The marina manager was still there and told me that the only thing left to do is pay him. He pushed an itemized bill across a worn blue Formica countertop for me to review. At first I thought that I was going to have to sign the boat over to them!

"$1,716,047 !" I yelled.

"Wait!" Said Lisa. That's only . . . . $3414 American dollars.

"Okay . . . . wooooooo!" I pulled out the American Express as he smiled at Lisa.

*　*　*

First thing Thursday morning they put it back in the water and connected it to a mooring buoy away from the commercial area. Lisa had to go to a local clothes supplier. I wanted to do a sea trial on the Saborio, and did not want to go by myself. I drank another cup of coffee at the kitchen table. About that time, Andres Jimenez pulled in. He came into the kitchen and joined me at the table. Momma poured him a cup of coffee. He shook his head from the strong Amaretto taste.

"I've got used to it!" I said, and laughed at him.

"I usually don't even drink coffee!" He confessed.

"Hey Andres . . . have you ever sailed?" I asked.

"No! But I have run a lot of fishing boats." He boasted.

"Would you like to help me take the Saborio out in a little while for a test run with the rebuilt keel?" I asked.

"Momma! Do you need me for anything today?" He asked her.

"No! You kids go have some fun!" She said.

"Looks like it's you and me!" He smiled and tried another drink of his Amaretto Coffee.

Lisa had our car, so Andres volunteered his for the trip to the marina. It only took about ten minutes. We went into the marina and parked the car in the back lot away from the office. We found the dingy on the dingy dock and sorted out the tangled dock lines that were all intertwined. My Honda outboard started on the first pull and we idled to the back porch of the Saborio. Andres was amazed when we went aboard.

"I have never seen a boat so beautiful! I could live on this for the rest of my life!" He said.

"I probably WILL live on it for most of mine!"

I started the diesel and let it idle.

"Go forward and untie the mooring!" I requested.

I let the wind push us away from the mooring ball until we were a safe distance from it and pushed the throttle forward. She responded fine under power and we gracefully left the marina.

Andres showed me a few faster ways to get into blue water and after ten minutes we were ready to raise sails. I had Andres hold us on course while I unfurled the jenny and then raised the main. I saw his face get worried when the giant boat heeled over and caught some air. I went back, killed the diesel, and set another course as I pointed to a cloud in the sky.

"Just keep her pointing to that cloud!"

I ran up onto the cabin and made some adjustments to the main.

"Are you ready to sail!" I yelled to Andres.

"YES!" His excitement grew.

I climbed back into the cockpit and started winching in the Jenny as the vessel heeled to 45 deg. The bow came up and dropped into the next wave followed by a ten foot high spray that came across the deck and splashed against the sails.

"WOOOOOOO!" Screamed Andres.

"Do you want to keep sailing?" I asked.

"Oh Yeah! WOOOOOOOO!"

His eyes were the size of silver dollars, and his stance was that of a Hockey Goalie guarding the net. He leaned excessively to Port as the boat listed to Starboard.

I rechecked his course and made an adjustment to the helm.

"That cloud right .... *there!*" as he studied where I was pointing.

He played ... and held the course, while I went below and cracked open two cold Imperial Beers from the cooler. I handed one to *Captain Jimenez* and sat back watching him being as happy as a child while I drank mine. I wasn't sure if he was going to let me sail or not? He had not even noticed that we had sailed out of sight of land, until I told him to bring her into the wind so we could tack.

"It's time to take her home." I said.

He handled her well when I yelled how much course change I needed, and when I needed it. He studied how I handled the sails but did not want to try to tack .... yet. He got worried when he found out that there was no land in site. I punched a few buttons on the chart plotter and showed him how it would plot a course directly back to the mooring buoy.

We were running partially down wind and things were getting a bit more complicated. Andres was ready to give up the helm. It was a slow, smooth, trip and he laughed about how I steered with my bare feet as I laid back with my beer. I think I have totally destroyed this man now.

When we got within clear sight of the marina, I started breaking down the sails and started the diesel. I let Andres take it in and he pulled it up to the buoy, and came to a dead stop like a pro.

Lisa and Loren were sitting on the dock watching us as I tied her off and covered the main.

Andres snapped down the hatch covers and pulled the dingy in for our departure. We motored in and both received affectionate kisses from our women. I was doing a double check to make sure we had the right ones.

Lisa was driving her car, but before Andres and Loren walked out to his, he pulled me off to the side and wanted to ask me a question.

"Hey Jonah! Would you care if Loren and I used your boat for a few hours later on tonight?"

"No problem! Just leave it like you got it!"

I handed him the keys to the companionway lock.

Lisa and I drove slowly back to the house as we talked about leaving Costa Rica. The boat was the only thing holding us here and it was ready to go. Lisa was going to turn in her notice to Bello Fashions and I will call the clothing manufacturer for final connections. We should be ready to go by next weekend. We offered to take Momma Saborio out sailing but after talking to Andres, she was, *too scared!*

All five of us sat around the table and ate baked fish on rice, while we exchanged stories.

Momma's psychic abilities were tuned like a guitar string. Andres and Loren had to go run an errand after supper .... and she immediately started grilling Lisa and I.

"But ! You knew we had to go back after the repairs to the boat were completed!" Said Lisa.

"Yes ... but I thought maybe you would just decide to keep it here, and stay in Costa Rica." She said sadly.

"Momma! I really like it here with you," I said, "but I have a home and a job in America. If I don't get back to work for my publisher, he might fire me! I am supposed to be signing books and answering questions from readers. It is in my contract that I have to help the advertising department any time they want me to. It's a good life, but sometimes I still have to work."

She shook her head. "I understand."

She went into the living room and sat on the couch. We went with her and watched the Tuesday Night Movie, in Spanish, until she went to bed.

As we sat with our foreheads together, talking quietly, we heard a car door slam out in front. Loren came in the house and headed for the shower. After her shower she came out wrapped in a towel. She walked past Lisa, came over and hugged me, then kissed me on the neck, and slid the boat keys into my hand.

"*Thanks!*" as she smiled at me and went to bed.

"What did she say?" Asked Lisa.

"Oh . . . She just thanked me for taking Andres sailing" I said casually.

Chapter 6

Once again we became the Bradford Yacht *Detail* Crew. We pulled all the cushions and cleaned it like a new boat. We stocked groceries and topped off all the tanks including the propane.

We were able to get Momma to come on board after we put it on the dock, *as long as we did not move it.* She loved it and said it was *more pretty then her house.* She inspected everything. She kept telling us we were rich, and she really liked the central air conditioning.

We said our final goodbyes to everyone. We took advantage of a break in the weather, and prepared to leave ahead of some rain that was coming in from the south this weekend.

"We will see you after hurricane season!"

I yelled, as we motored away from the dock.

After a few hours of quiet and depression, Lisa started getting excited about the challenge that I described to her. The thought of being independently wealthy from her own business, was becoming more real than her shrinking bank account. I explained to her how to get financing without spending our own money and she was listening intently.

We made a few long stops to maintain our sanity, but still managed to cover 1600 miles in 32 days. We had a few nasty storms and a few pirate scares that were false alarms, but the initial trip from Costa Rica to Jamaica was the worst. We had rough ocean waves most of the way and by the time we saw Haiti on the Horizon, I was wishing that I had bought an airline ticket. Lisa had got seasick a few times and I had some rough symptoms when we first left Limon.

We had to limit our time ashore. After being on the ocean so long, standing on the hard, made us feel sick. I guess we will recondition later, but for now we decided to continue on the ocean. It smoothed out once we started stopping more often and we gradually became more acclimated to the solid ground. By the time we saw Florida we were as good as new and feeling like we could do it again .... *maybe not?*

We cleared into customs in West Palm Beach, and continued up the coast for the next two days.

We put the Saborio on a transient mooring on the ICW and took the dingy into our marina. The Beneteau was still at the dock and I caught myself checking for the Nordhaven Trawler that started this entire adventure. I called a taxi to take us home and decided to go get my truck at the airport tomorrow.

Lisa ran a hot bathtub to soak her body in baby oil. I stood in the Master Bath shower until the water temperature started dropping. We both ended up back in my big bed and did not get up until noon the following day.

*　　*　　*

We picked up the truck at the Orlando Airport off grounds parking area, bought groceries, and paid the bills that were not on auto-pay. After that, we basically did not leave the house for the next week. We slept a lot and researched setting up a franchise on the internet. In the end we decided to involve a good attorney from Orlando that used to represent most of the banks in Florida. That was the best idea we had, seeing how he worked the investments from both sides for us. We rented a shop in downtown Orlando that was in the traffic pattern from the bars and the tourist shopping areas. While I built the flashy store interior and the logo for the sign, Lisa flew back to Costa Rica. She shipped several large containers of clothing by airfreight to the store. We were almost ready for the grand opening. I had talked to a TV advertiser about running commercials for us but I wanted to wait for Lisa to get back to see how *she* wanted to advertise it?

When I was in Costa Rica, Loren had very long hair and Lisa's was just a bit past her shoulders. Lisa dressed like a model most of the time and Loren dressed like local people with a uniform to work in. Even though they were twins, it was still fairly easy to tell one from the other.

Friday evening Lisa was coming in at OIA at 9:45 on a flight from Miami. I did this pick up all the time and tonight decided to sit in the airport cell phone lot and wait until she called me.

"Hi Jonah . . . This is Lisa! I'm ready when you are!"

I started the motor and drove out of the sand lot across to the pick-up area. I bounced across a huge speed bump and into an empty spot along the sidewalk. Lisa waved from the curb. I rolled up to her, and shut off the Cherokee. She walked up to me as I raised the hatch and put her luggage into the back. She turned and kissed me on the lips as I pulled her hips against me with both hands. I held her tightly and looked into her eyes. She smiled at me as if she had a surprise.

"What are you up to?" I asked.

She pushed her head against my chest and placed her hand on my butt.

Lisa . . . came through the exit door and walked toward the Cherokee. She smiled and walked up to me, and pulled the girl out of my arms.

"Get your own!"

They both giggled and Loren got into the back seat, while Lisa practically made love to me in the parking lane.

"We were having fun." She said. "We got our hair done exactly the same, and bought identical clothes. Even our panties are the same!" More giggling.

"Show me!" I said.

"Later!" Said Loren, as the giggling continued.

We took Rt. 528 back to the Space Coast while Loren looked into the darkness of the wetlands along the road. She ended up laid over in the seat sleeping with her head on her flight bag. Her dress rode up to her hip with her feet against the door. I periodically glanced into the back checking the status of her tan legs.

Lisa kept her hand on my thigh and rubbed my neglected *member*. She smiled at me from the occasional lift . . . . as it tried to decide if we were going to battle, or not?

Finally arriving home, we pulled the luggage into the foyer and got the boxes of display samples from the Jeep. Lisa took Loren down the hallway and showed her the room that I had quickly prepared for her. I followed and lifted her big bag onto the far side of the king sized bed.

Lisa pulled Loren's door shut as we exited.

Lisa began hanging her clothes in the closet. She pulled her dress off, and was running around the master bedroom in her new white lace panties.

"So, are Loren's panties the same as yours?" I asked.

"Same design, but hers are black." as she crawled up onto my bed and slid under the covers.

With both girls out for the night, I checked the door locks and hit the remotes for the cars. I joined Lisa in my room. She woke long enough to move across the big bed, put her head on my shoulder, and squeeze me.

"I missed you sooo bad." She said softly as she left the real world.

Lisa was up early and was covering's Momma's duties. She made breakfast and a pot of coffee. I entered the kitchen and she told me how much she liked the kitchen design and the black granite counter tops.

"So?" . . . . Lisa said, "You built this kitchen yourself?"

Loren appeared against a wall behind me.

"Yes!" I said, "It's all solid Cherry with a lot of fancy extras."

Loren rubbed her eyes and staggered toward the coffee pot as Lisa got a cup from the cabinet.

We each put our breakfast on a tray and carried it into the living room to watch the Channel 9 News on the big screen TV. I sat in my robe and both girls wore white T-shirts. There was nothing but bare legs coming out from under the trays.

They both wanted to see what I had done to the new shop. After we ate, I couldn't get near a bathroom. Lisa was in mine and Loren was already calling the hallway bath hers.

I had to stretch over Lisa to shave, while we talked.

"So . . . when did you decide to bring Loren?"

"A few days ago! The Avis rental car company is being bought out by another company. They let everyone go, and are going to re-hire new employees. They will re-hire a few of the original employees. Loren does not think she will get called back in, and I could use her help getting things going in the store." She said with excitement.

"Yeah, Good idea! I bet your Mother is pissed!"

"Oh yeah! Loren broke up with Andres before we left. Momma doesn't even have Andres now!" Lisa said sadly.

"Wow! So is Loren going to try to stay in Florida?" I asked.

"She's going to try! Bama has a new "*Welcome to America*" program so we should be able to get citizenship easier."

I had not realized how attached I had become to Mrs. Saborio. I worried about her being alone in Costa Rica.

The girls dressed differently this time, and we left for Orlando. When they talked, you could detect a bit of difference in their speech. This was Loren's first time out of Costa Rica and Lisa had traveled to several different countries. You could hear the influence.

Loren had her face against the glass as we came into Orlando. She had never seen wealth as prominently displayed like it is in America. After living here my entire life, I did not see it as rich, impressive, and clean, until after I lived in Costa Rica and saw it through their eyes. They wanted the dream to come true and I was going to do everything I could to make it happen.

A lot of the business still had to be setup in my name because Lisa was not American. I kept her name on as much as I could for her security and also for the logo name. We spent a lot of money on the Grand Opening and took another delivery of intimate apparel from the manufacturer in Costa Rica. He claimed this was a hot line of product in Europe and no one was marketing it in the US yet.

*   *   *

The day of the opening Lisa was a wreck. She was nervous and often exploded in anger at me. Loren would drag me from the room and explain that;

"Lisa is always like this when she gets stressed. She will be okay after a few sales." She reassured me.

We opened the doors at 8:00 and didn't have a single customer show up until 10:30. I explained to her that people run a little different schedule in Florida and maybe we could adjust the hours once we see a pattern.

Lisa immediately became a gracious host and welcomed all of her new customers. As they left with their purchases, I passed out discount coupons for their next visit, in an attempt to establish return customers. Loren roamed the shop, assisted and advised. People had to only look at her appearance to know they could trust her opinion. It seemed to be working and the money was coming in.

At the end of the day we had made a big dent in the designer clothing and almost sold out of the intimate apparel. We placed another order by phone and told them to expedite the shipping.

We kept the shop open through Saturday. We were all exhausted and were glad to just crash out on Sunday.

We went into the second week, and I let the girls run with it. I stayed home, cut the grass, and listed the Beneteau with a local Yacht Broker. I moved the Beneteau to his office docks for a fast sale. I brought the Saborio in to a large dock with electric for the air conditioner, and re-established my floating office deduction.

One day I was sitting at the galley table typing my manuscript. I realized I was using a lot of the experiences from Costa Rica in my writing. It just so happened that I was using situations from momma's house, and I found myself wondering how she was doing. I picked up my cell phone and called her. She said she had been paying the kid that mowed her grass to drive her to the grocery and do her running. Momma still paid all her bills in person. She didn't trust the mail and didn't even know how to turn on a computer. She said that Andres still dropped in once in a while for breakfast but he had a new girlfriend named Macy and was talking about getting married. The more I heard her broken English and her old world opinions, the more I missed her.

"Momma . . . Would you like to see Lisa's store?" I asked.

"Oh yes!" She said excitedly.

"If I send you a ticket, would you like to visit America for a week or two?"

"Oh yes . . . grande mucho!" She said.

"Let me see what I can do, *and you get ready.*" I could almost see her big smile right through the phone.

"Okay! . . . . Jonah?" She sounded worried.

"Yes!"

"I've never been on a plane." She said.

"Don't worry . . . just ask questions? Go to any desk or flight attendant. Most of them can speak Spanish."

Two weeks later I had her arriving at OIA. I told the girls that I had a conference call with my editor and publicist, and I was going to stay home today. I drove to the airport and met Momma Saborio on the Florida side of the Customs desk. We recovered her luggage, and headed to the fashion shop for an unexpected joke.

We left her bags in the car and I had her walk in and act as if she was interested in some lingerie. Lisa walked up behind her.

"Can I help you Mam?"

"Momma started talking in Spanish and I thought Lisa was going to hit the floor. I laughed myself breathless. Loren came out of the back room and the whole place ignited in Spanish and hugging. I got no credit for my effort until later that evening at home.

One thing I had not compensated for was three Costa Rican women in my little Florida house.

I decided that while momma was here, Lisa and I would sleep on the boat. The marina was only about ten minutes up Rt.1, and the boat had two bathrooms, too. With the tension that Lisa was bringing home every night, she needed mental and physical relief. I made sure that her tension level remained under control. If she was in melt down mode, we motored out into the Intercostal Waterway and went south to one of the little sandbar islands. We could play on the island and the beaches until she was exhausted, and then sleep in air-conditioned luxury in the Saborio. This also allowed *Loren* to spend some quality time with momma.

Lisa hired a manager trainee for this store and Loren took momma sightseeing. They explored this side of Florida and bought things that they cannot get in Costa Rica. The highlight of her days of shopping was when Loren and momma found Disney World. They each came home with mouse ears on their heads and a photo of them with Goofy. I had given Loren my credit card and told her not to go crazy. Loren was very responsible and stayed below the spending limit that I gave her.

She had been driving the Cherokee while Lisa and I used the truck. While I felt right at home in my little Nissan, Lisa kept singing the theme song to "*Green Acres*" and snickering.

* * *

We were getting regular scheduled shipments from the Island Sea Freight Company now. They delivered to the back door of the shop by truck as part of the price. My job was to unload the container while the girls inventoried and checked every item. Once the container was empty, I could go home.

A few weeks later, Loren took Momma Saborio to the airport with a few extra bags of gifts and goodies. She felt better knowing where her girls were and that they were happy. Momma missed her house and her friends at her church. She was anxious to get home, and I think the fast pace of the United States was getting to her.

With the new manager trainee finally getting the operations down, Lisa added another girl that was hired primarily because she liked the way she dressed. The new hire was a bit radical, and seemed to attract a lot of the younger clientele. As the younger clients came in to buy the new styles from her, she would also initiate them into lingerie and expanded their boyfriend's options. We dropped into the shop, un-announced several times a week, and checked the books on weekends.

While the girls made the money, I set up a server that monitored the entire inventory as it was bought and sold. It also kept a running balance of the store operations. I could sit on the boat, check the store accounts, and see it in real time through the audio/video monitors. It worked so well that I suggested that we open another store in Melbourne, Florida.

Lisa was not sure she wanted to. She liked the one store, one headache scenario, and seemed afraid of going viral. She needed a break and some time to let the idea soak in. Lisa and Loren had both passed their allowable passport time and had working Visa's now. I had an application in to sponsor them both on green cards, but the process was dragging along slowly due to more Bama changes. They were doing a thorough investigation on me; to be sure I wasn't pimping them out or something?

We decided to let the store run solo for a few weeks and the three of us packed for a way overdue trip to the Bahamas.

Chapter 7

O nce again we topped off all the tanks of the Saborio. We made sure the license and insurance were up to date, motored down the ICW, and through the locks past Blue Point. I hated this part of the trip. The sand bars are always shoaling and the wind is too inconsistent to turn off the diesel. Even with my modified keel, I still had to have a six-foot bottom depth to operate. Once we cleared the Disney Boat and the Carnival Condos, the feeling of freedom returned to the Saborio and we were almost as excited as when I took Andres out. Lisa had become a good sailor, and we were jointly teaching Loren.

"Just keep her pointing to that cloud!" Said Lisa, as she smiled at me.

The twins were laughing again, and we were all starting to relax. All of our tans had lightened and we were all working on them while we sailed. I was the official sunburn monitor, and responsible for dispersing the proper PH number as required. *I loved my job.*

While they took turns sailing, I rubbed lotion on both of their bodies as the sun cooked it in. I didn't just apply sun-block, but rubbed it in like a massage. They occasionally instructed me as to which areas required additional attention, and I followed instruction proficiently.

As the Saborio leaped through the waves, an occasional spray would mist across the deck cooling us off. There was a pod of dolphins that had been running with us off the port bow for the last half hour. I locked on the autopilot and we all watched them and took photos.

The sun started to set behind us, so we discussed the night shifts and sleeping arrangements. As great as the master cabin was, it was a lousy arrangement for open water. It had a centerline queen size bed and you rolled back and forth and occasionally into the floor. In the V-berth the bed was on the port side and was more contained. It even had a net that slid from under the mattress that maintained your body on the bed. It was getting dark, so I checked the chart plotter and tweaked our course for the evening. I wanted to avoid the commercial zones and shallow areas. I agreed to take the last watch, and relinquished the helm to Loren. I went below and crawled into the V-berth. I was out in ten minutes and Lisa and Loren stayed on deck. The water calmed down, and Lisa wanted to get some sleep before she had to go on watch in another ninety minutes. She crawled into the V-berth next to me and laid her head on my shoulder. I felt her head and leg get heavier as her breathing increased. The V-berth hatch was open and the air was getting cooler so I threw the sheet across us both to contain our body heat. Lisa was wearing a bikini under a T-shirt. I slid my hand under the T-shirt and under the back of her bottoms, *as I often do*, then went back to sleep.

Later Loren locked off the autopilot and came below to say her shift was over. Lisa and Loren went back up on deck and discussed the details of the last two hours. Lisa released the autopilot and locked in the tether to the vest that Loren helped her put on.

Loren came back down into the V-berth and slid under the sheets with me. I rolled onto my back. She laid her head on my shoulder and her leg across my torso. I ran my hand back under her shirt and under the back of her bottoms, *as usual*, and went back to sleep. As the boat rocked through the waves, she rolled onto her back and I, onto my side facing her. This drug my hand from the back of her bottoms to the front and I felt her pubic area. She made a quiet little moan.

I was awake now and continued rubbing, which caused her to jump and twitch. She was getting closer to climax. She pulled my face over to hers, kissing me passionately, until she had finished. She replaced her head on my shoulder and her hand on my enlarged member then went back to sleep. I was awakened by Lisa's touch.

"Your turn!" She whispered.

I carefully climbed over Loren who was quietly snoring. I went on deck with Lisa and she briefed me on where we were and what she had seen. I locked in the tether and turned the autopilot off. Lisa went below and crawled into bed with her sister.

As I watched out over the big black ocean I fantasized about having them both, and wondered what the repercussions would be if I was shared?

With my testosterone activated, I was not sleepy anymore and sailed through the rest of the night. I could see the sun starting to glow from below the horizon, and could make out a few lights of the island through my binoculars. I heard the girls giggling from the V-berth and could only wonder what they may be talking about as they occasionally looked around the cabin wall and smiled at me. Lisa was the first on deck. She brought me a coffee and thanked me for letting her sleep.

I drank my coffee and showed her how far we had come since her watch. You could see the island now, and again I reset the chart plotter so I could go to sleep for a bit. The girls ran the boat in their bikinis, while the PH Monitor snored in the V-berth.

I was amazed later to find out that the girls had dropped the sails and set the anchor on a shoal that was close to the big island without waking me up. I must have really been tired. They had found a big inflatable mattress in the storage and the two of them had blown it up. They had tied it to the back of the boat and were floating on it.

I had pulled out the sun shade on the hatch, and someone had closed the cabin door so it was still moderately dark in the cabin so I could sleep. I woke partially when I felt a hand on my unit. My shorts were then unzipped and removed. I felt a warm naked body sit on me. It was a great wet dream, *or maybe not,* seeing how I woke up naked with my shorts smashed against the bottom of the bed under the sheets. I got dressed and went up on deck watching the girls pushing each other off of the air mattress into the clear water. I studied them both, trying to guess who was in my cabin. They each displayed a childish smile. I sat back against the cabin and whispered to myself.

"It doesn't really matter. I am such a lucky guy!"

I then jumped into the water and swam for the air mattress.

*   *   *

After lunch we motored the Saborio into the tourist area while Lisa called ahead on the VHF and reserved dock space for a 46' cutter with a deep keel. I backed it in and we tied her off like we knew what we were doing. All the dockhands watched in admiration as I bumped the bow thruster and brought her right into place like a pro. They may have also been impressed with the two beautiful Cost Rican girls in bikinis that bent and stretched while tying her off.

I don't know?

I instructed them to go put on land clothes, and we left in search of a grocery. We restocked the food supply, and the girls wanted to go study local fashions to send to Costa Rica for replication. They sat in an open-air restaurant where they could watch the styles from other boats, and tourists from other countries.

I sat in the cockpit with my laptop on my legs typing about the smells and activities that I was experiencing and how my main character had an;

**Unusual wet dream, with the twin daughters,
of a Voodoo woman from Haiti.**

We went out to supper at the *Boom-Boom Room.* The food was fantastic and the waitress's dresses were split to the top of their hips. When you leave a tip, you personally place it in the G-string that shows from the split in her dress.

We hung out on this island for two days and then found a quiet island that was uninhabited. It was big enough to explore, and we anchored in 15 feet of water. We built sand castles and the girls buried me in the sand then dug me out one piece at a time. They tickled me and threatened to arouse me then leave me to be sun burnt.

There were conch everywhere here and I brought up enough for a meal. I showed the twins how to make conch soup in our little onboard pressure cooker. I mixed a pitcher of Painkillers and we were all unconscious in the master cabin by 1AM. I woke up about 4AM to use the head and looked back and forth at the two beauties beside me. I got back in bed and they were still asleep. I had a face on both of my shoulders, and a pair of T-shirt covered breasts pressed into each side of my chest.

When I woke up, Loren was sleeping in *her* cabin.

Lisa buried her chin into my chest and was staring at me.

"About time you woke up!" as she smiled.

I rolled over, held her face gently in my hands, and kissed her.

"I love you Lisa Saborio."

Her kiss became more passionate!

* * *

We made one more stop on an even smaller island and Lisa came back with some local clothing.

She drew on them with magic markers, making lines and arrows, explaining what she wanted to change. She had accumulated a fairly large pile of clothing that she wanted to send to Costa Rica for modification or replication. She also found some new fabrics and designs.

The vacation was over and everyone was considerably more relaxed than when it started. We left the Bahamas on the pre-aylight tide and sailed out into the darkness. Once again we put in our shifts at the helm.

I was still at the helm when the girls brought breakfast up on deck and set up the cockpit table. I kicked the helm over onto autopilot long enough to enjoy my breakfast. No one wanted to sleep during the day and as we neared sunset, my energy level was running low. Once again I headed for the V-berth. The girls took turns sleeping in the cockpit and switching back and forth at the helm allowing me to sleep most of the evening. When I woke up in the morning they were both exhausted and climbed into the V-berth as I calculated set and drift for the Gulfstream.

I waved at a Caribbean Cruise ship as their passengers hung over the safety rails watching us pound through the waves. Cape Canaveral was in sight now and I turned the autopilot on again and took my time bringing down the sails. When I started the diesel, Lisa and Loren appeared on deck ready to help wherever they could.

I preferred to take the boat through the locks by myself. Sometimes the currents would do weird things to, *how the boat handles,* in there. We backed into our slip about four hours later and loaded all of our bootie into the back of the Cherokee. Lisa was anxious to get her new product lines delivered to Costa Rica and said she wanted to deliver them herself and spend a few days with momma while she was there. I got my mail from the mailbox and found two envelopes from immigration. Lisa and Loren had both been approved to be sponsored by myself. Now they both could stay in the United States legally as long as I continued as their sponsor.

* * *

Lisa boxed up her clothing and headed for Costa Rica two days after we got home. She was definitely a woman on a mission focusing on her specialized clothing line.

While she was out of the country, Loren and I met with a realtor friend of mine from Merritt Island. He lined us up several commercial properties that were located in areas that would support a fashion outlet. We spent days going through empty buildings and strip store locations. We finally decided on one of the more expensive options that he showed us in an area called Viera. It was a growing area of specialized upper class shops that we felt would bring the type clientele that would desire Lisa's product. We signed the contract, applied for permits, and started remodeling the store in the same style as the one in Orlando. I had a duplicate sign created and it would be installed within 30 days. We covered the storefront windows with paper while we were working. I was impressed at how helpful Loren was while I built walls and hung drywall on them. No matter what I did, she was always right there handing me the next tool or holding the other end of the board.

One night we worked until seven o'clock. We got in my truck and headed North on I-95. I called Cracker Barrel from my cell phone and ordered two dinners to go. I remained in the truck while Loren ran into the restaurant and picked up the order. As we sat on the couch watching the TV and eating our food I occasionally looked at what she was eating. I stabbed it with my fork and tried it. She would take her fork and stab mine and before long we were both eating off of both plates and food was falling on our laps and on the couch. I picked up some baby carrots off of the couch, pushed them against her chest, watching them fall down into her shirt. She squealed from the feeling then scooped up the rest of my mashed potatoes, crammed them up the leg of my shorts, smashing them around my unit. This became war. I found my unopened container of biscuit gravy and she grabbed the grits. The clothes were saturated and the couch was going to require a professional cleaning. We laughed as we ran down the hall together with food falling onto the Persian rug as we went. We jumped into the walk in shower of the master bedroom fully dressed. We stood with the water running, the food falling, and grabbed the shampoo from the towel bar.

We both washed our hair and used the shampoo to clean our clothing. As the suds rinsed away I started unbuttoning her blouse, and let the carrots fall into the shower. The laughing stopped. Within 60 seconds we both stood naked in the shower with our squeaky-clean bodies in full contact. After a rapid towel dry, the activities moved into the bedroom and continued until after midnight.

We woke up in the morning holding onto each other in my bed. I was wondering what I had done now, and how it was going to end up. I was in love with Lisa, but she has become so obsessed with her business, that the qualities that I used to like about Lisa have now become more prominent in Loren.

I gave Loren the keys to the Cherokee and had her go to Orlando and work with the new girl today. I felt guilty about being with her, and if she stays here with me . . . I'll probably do it again. I also needed to re-evaluate my feelings for Lisa . . . and Loren.

The next day we both went back to Viera and continued working on the new store. Loren and I still laughed and had a good time but we tried not to touch each other knowing where it would end up. We worked late and came home dirty, and tired.

The night before Lisa came home; Loren came into my bedroom and lay on the bed next to me.

"Jonah . . . . don't be worried about what happened between us. I will never say a word about it to Lisa. I know you are in love with her and she is in love with you, but I have needs too and somehow being around you makes them worse. I wish I could be Lisa, but I can see that is not going to happen. I will wait a week or two after Lisa gets home, and go back to Costa Rica. Does this sound like I have a fairly clear picture of the situation?" She whispered.

"Unfortunately . . . . it does." I said.

I rolled over in the bed and kissed her gently on the lips and lay back down on my back.

"Jonah . . . Lisa will not be home until tomorrow evening. Could it make anything any worse to spend another night with me before she arrives?" She asked.

"I don't think that . . . ." and she put her hand over my mouth and pushed her hot body against mine. It was an exhausting and very satisfying evening.

Once again I woke up with her clinging to me as the sun shined through my bedroom window. I quietly got up, made two omelets, and put a pot of coffee on before she woke up. I took the tray with the breakfast on it into the bedroom and served her where she lay.

"I am really going to miss you Jonah." She said sadly.

"I am going to miss you too!"

I gently kissed her and finished my breakfast.

"NOW! I need you to help me clean up this house and change the sheets on the bed . . . okay?"

"*I'm on it Captain*! Am I allowed to put on some clothes first?" as she giggled.

"NO!"

I smacked her buns and took the tray back into the kitchen.

Chapter 8

I picked up Lisa at the airport by myself and we talked on the way back. She told me that while she was at momma's, Andres had stopped over and ask about Loren.

"He really misses her and wants her back badly." She said.

"Well that's strange, Loren helped me on the new store and she told me that she plans to go back to Costa Rica in the near future."

"Tomorrow we will drive down to Viera and I will show you the new store. It is in a premium location and we are probably within a couple weeks of being able to open. Do you have enough product coming to stock another store?" I ask.

"Oh yes . . . . and there's going to be lot of original creations in this load. I worked with their designers while I was there and showed them exactly what I wanted. We even bought the fabric that I want to use."

She smiled and squeezed my leg.

* * *

The next morning we drove to the new store. Lisa loved the location and they just so happened to be installing the Saborio Fashions, sign when we arrived. Her face was lit up like a child with a new toy, and it made me feel really good that she was so happy with my choice of locations. The inventory arrived two weeks later. We really missed Loren after unloading the sea container by ourselves. A few days afterwards we advertised the grand opening and it started producing more income than the original store. These rich women in this neighborhood just could not get enough.

"I wish Loren had stayed long enough to see this!" Said Lisa.

*   *   *

By the time we were seeing steady cash flow and had trained a store manager, Lisa and I were in need of another vacation. This time we decided to fly to Costa Rica and stay in a luxury mountain home near the volcano. Every few days we would go drop in on momma and Loren, but then we would escape back to our private mountain home.

Loren had reconciled with Andres and they were looking like a couple again. It sort of removed the temptation that I still felt, and at the same time made me jealous when I saw them playing and acting silly. Lisa had talked to Loren from Florida, so we were aware of their situation, but seeing them in person put the salt peter to it.

Andre acted differently toward me. We were still good friends, but I felt something deeper, between the lines, as we talked. I had to wonder if Loren told him about us.

Loren and Andres announced that they were going to be married soon. Andres confided in Lisa and I that Loren was going to have his baby. Momma knew that they were going to get married and was very excited about it, but she did not know anything about the baby and they were not going to tell her until after they had been married for a little while. They did not want mama to get the ridicule from all of her churchy friends. Momma became a wedding planner as she recruited several of her church friends and planned to cook and sew for her *second-born* daughter's wedding. She had talked to the minister and was making Loren and Andres attend Sunday meetings with her in preparation.

* * *

Loren and I laid on our mountain patio in a double recliner and watched the sun setting over Western Costa Rica. We watched the profiles of the giant wind generators slowly turning in front of the orange and magenta skies behind them.

"Lisa . . . . do you love me?" I asked seriously.

"That's a stupid question . . . you know I do. I have loved you from the time we left that cheap hotel on the south end of Okeechobee Lake." She stated.

"How would you feel about loving me for the rest of your life?" I asked.

She swung her legs up onto the recliner and sat cross-legged studying my face.

"What are you saying?" She asked.

"Will you marry me and be with me forever until you have to use me for an anchor?" I ask with a small whim of a smile.

"She broke out laughing and crying at the same time as she hugged me and repeated . . . yes . . . yes . . . yes, yes, yes, yes!"

She hugged me in a death grip and whispered into my ear as her tears ran onto my neck.

"You are the only person I have ever heard of that managed to incorporate his sailboat into a marriage proposal!" We both laughed and went back into the cottage.

While we sat on the couch watching another movie in Spanish, I had another thought.

"What do you think about sharing a wedding with Loren and Andres? Do you think that they would be interested in that idea? It would knock momma right off her feet!" We both laughed some more.

Two weeks later we all four got married in momma's church. I had never seen her look so proud as both of her daughters walked down the aisles to their prospective husbands. There was a few last minute glimpses between Loren and I, but in the end we smiled at each other and were pleased with the choices that we had made. There was a large reception for us that had been prepared behind the church. Tiki lights were everywhere as was the food and drinks. Some of the church members had a band and played on the back deck. Most of the people danced and laughed. I ... *who can't dance* ... even finally had enough liquor that I danced too. I probably looked ridiculous, but we all had a good time.

The women had brought in tall vases with flowers that grow locally and had them sitting at the base of the lanterns. Toward the end of the evening, they gathered the flowers and divided them between Lisa, Loren, and even a few for momma.

They demanded that the newlyweds leave, and they would take care of the cleanup. Momma had a great group of friends, and now they felt like our friends. Lisa and Loren went inside and changed from their beautiful white wedding gowns that the women created for them, into short dresses. Andres and I took off our ties and jackets. Lisa and I got into our black BMW rental from Avis, and Loren and Andres got into their Subaru wagon with the paint peeling. Lisa and I headed for the mountain home, and weren't seen for the rest of the week. I was good at pretending to be a newlywed. My imagination developed scenarios for all kinds of crazy sex for honeymooners. After the tourists went back to their hotels ... we went roaming the mountains. Lisa will never look at the volcano the same way again. Our time here was coming to an end, and I was getting antsy about returning to Florida.

Lisa and I paid the rent for our mountain home for another week, and handed the keys to Loren and Andres as a gift. They would not have had the money for such a nice extended honeymoon and it made us feel good to supply it for them. We hugged everyone and said our goodbyes. They delivered us to the airport and waved to us as we went through customs as Mr. and Mrs. Bradford.

* * *

We put Lisa's green card in the scrapbook for memory purposes. We mortgaged the house, and the boat, and built three more *Saborio Fashions* stores. They were getting a reputation as a high-end Veronika's Secret type store. We found that by quadrupling our sales price, the public felt they were getting something better. Little did they know that the price was already doubled from what we paid as soon as it landed in North America. We paid off the house and had the lien removed from the sailboat. We started selling franchises all across the US. We sold Lisa's designs over the Internet in 22 different countries, and now every piece that she sold had a Saborio label sewn into it. We hardly ever set foot in the stores anymore leaving our attorneys to take care of the majority of the franchise accounts. We just had to show up every so often to sign documents.

My last book that I sent the publisher also became a bestseller. They decided to market it globally and even produced it as an e-book for immediate download. Life was good!

*   *   *

I was content with my Hylas 46. I had the money now to buy any boat that I could possibly want but this one was just fine.

I decided that it was time to get out of this little flat Florida house that we had been using for a base for the last few years. I called my realtor buddy, Jack, again, and had him look for a medium-size home with a dock or seawall and deep water ocean access. I was getting tired of spending $50 in diesel fuel and hours of my sailing time just to get out on the blue water.

He found several homes that fit my description but almost all of them were more expensive than I wanted to pay. Finally he called me all excited!

"Jonah! I think I just found your house. The customer just came to me to list it and it's not even on the MLS service yet. It needs a lot of work but that's your thing . . . . Right!"

It's got a seawall and a custom deep-water dock connected to a swimming pool. You can get on the ocean in ten minutes, and it is a four bedroom, four baths, with a three-car garage. The carpet is shot and the cabinets are dated. The people had not made any interior changes since 1985 but it is all cosmetic. Are you interested?" Ask Jack.

"Where's it at?"

"Just outside of Stuart. Just south of Port St Lucie." He said.

"Make me an appointment! As soon as possible." I replied.

We looked at it two days later. It not only had the advertised goodies but it had a mother-in-law apartment above the garage completely separate from the house. The dock had been built in the last few years and that was the most important thing to me. The rest could be upgraded easily. The shrubs and trees had all been left to grow wild, but all these things were do-able. We wrote up an offer of $378,000 and they countered with $400,000. We met with them and settled for $385,000. That sounds like a real bargain for the area, but I would probably drop another $80,000 in it before I would be content. A lot of the furniture was still in the house and they agreed to leave it if we wanted it. Otherwise they had to pay someone else to haul it all away and they lived in Iowa. We agreed to keep it and also to close on the house thirty days later. I didn't want to make it final until I brought the Saborio down and made sure the access was deep enough, and the dock was a good fit. I wrote it into the contract as a contingency.

Our net worth was in the millions now as we continued selling franchises and writing more books. I even wrote one that explained how to become a millionaire by franchising. It made more money than my novels. We hired local contractors to attack the house while I had Jack start taking applications to use our old home as a rental property. Our upgrades were going to take quite a bit of time to complete, and cost a lot of money to bring it to the standards that we desire. By just moving the boat to Stuart it would save us $528 a month for the dock, and the insurance got cheaper because it was stored in our back yard.

We decided to have all the carpet removed and all the floors redone in marble. I had a Wenge Kitchen custom built by a small shop in Rockledge, and all the painting and faux finishes done by an old friend of mine that flew in from Montana. It was magazine grade when we were finished, and it was almost a shame to move into it. We had been staying in the boat most of the time anyway. We had not had a final inspection on the upgrades yet, and we could not get a commitment on when the inspector might show up. When he finally did show up he found an issue about the electrical amperage to our meter box being too low. With two HVAC systems and the new mother-in-law quarters, he wanted us to increase the house amperage to 300 amps, and install a completely separate meter for the apartment. We hired an electrician and decided to head back to Costa Rica.

*   *   *

Loren's son David was almost two years old now and we had only seen photos. He had strep throat a few times. Loren would get worried about it and have to talk to Lisa. They spent hours on the phone when David was sick. I think she just needed the security of her sister's voice.

Loren and Andres money was so tight that one time we called a doctor in Costa Rica and paid him with my credit card to cover David's doctor bill. Lisa seemed to know all about kids. I somehow had spent the majority of my life with adults. Even as a child, I was always surrounded by adults. It is not that I do not like children; it just somehow was always screened out of my life? All babies look like little Martians to me until they get hair and a personality. If they smell like BUTT, they belong to someone else!

*   *   *

Andres was working for CNFL Electric doing line work on the west coast. Loren had gone back to work at Avis Car Rental by the marina in Limon. Andres's job required him to be gone for weeks at a time running new utility lines across mountains and roads. We drove our rental car to momma's house and she was babysitting for David. He climbed right up on my lap as I sat on the couch and he showed me his toy sailboat that his mommy bought him. He listened intently as I explained how it leaned over, bounced up and down in the waves, and when his aunt Lisa drives, it goes *KerPlunk!* and sinks to the bottom of the ocean. He laughed and repeated . . . *KerPunk!*

Occasionally David lost me in his conversation. He had some things that he preferred to say in Spanish and others that were in perfect English, sometimes in the same sentence. He had light brown . . . almost blonde hair, and had a strong looking body for his age. He listened and watched things intently and seemed to be absorbing everything that he saw.

I found a bag of p-nut M&M's in the kitchen. I laid one under the edge of my shorts on the couch and showed David the M&M's in my hand. I picked out a red one, made a vacuum sound with my mouth, and inhaled the red M&M. I then closed my eyes and tensed my body as if I was trying to fart. I made a fart sound and pulled the red M&M from under my shorts.

"Grandma! Grandma! Uncle Jonah farted an M&M! His eyes were as big as quarters.

"Okay! Nap time" . . . Momma scooped him up and shook her head at me disgusted.

"That is how I am with kids. I am always getting in trouble." I tried to explain.

Lisa sat in the kitchen and had been watching me with David.

"You are good with children." She said with a strange twinkle in her eyes.

"It's easy if you never had to grow up." I said.

"That explains it!" She agreed.

Lisa had been sitting around talking to her mother all day and I was bored. David woke up from his nap and he wanted me to play. I was out of games and volunteered to take him fishing over at the canal. I grabbed a couple fishing rods off of the front porch, found some worms under some rotten boards, and headed for the canal. Most of the worms were small, but we added some grubs and bugs in case the fish were picky.

Andres had taken him fishing before and David was telling me what he knew, verses what I was doing. I baited his hook, cast it out into the middle of the canal, and handed David the rod. I baited mine too and cast it along the far side. We sat and watched our bobbers talking about what kids in North America do.

As the conversation got quieter and the concentration was on the fishing. I drifted off into the memories of how many times Lisa and I had crushed the grass beside that old wooden boat behind me. It seems that times were so much simpler then. It was only four or five years ago  but it seems more like ten. Between my books and the stores, we had enough money to never work again if we chose not to, but working had become an obsession, and we could not find the STOP button.

"Jonah! Jonah! I think I might have . . . ."

Suddenly David's bobber disappeared into a small tidal wave and the reel was spinning as we watched the waves heading away from us. He held the rod tightly as I slowly started reeling it in for him.

"Don't let go! He's wearing down!" I yelled and continued cranking.

"Hurry up Uncle Jonah! I'm getting tired!" He said all excited.

"Here . . . . I'll hold the rod and you crank it!" I suggested.

David gave up the rod and cranked a half revolution at a time. It took forever but we finally threw a huge catfish onto the bank while David checked it out.

"He's a big one!" I said, "He probably has a whole family of little fish down on the bottom! What do you want to do with him?"

"Put him back in! Keep him with his family!" He said very seriously.

I looked at him quite surprised and then held the catfish down with the toe of my shoe while I took the hook from his mouth.

I picked up a small board that was lying by the old boat and handed it to David.

"You better put him back in the water. He can't breathe air like us." I showed him the gills flapping in and out.

I helped David push the board under the catfish and flipped it through the air, watching intently as he splashed into the water and swam straight to the bottom. He turned and smiled at me proudly.

"Did he go home?"

"Oh yes! He's down there with his kids right now!" We packed up and went back to the house.

David would not let me alone about the M&M trick. He was insistent that I teach him how to do it. Finally while grandma was taking a nap, David and I sat on the couch and I got a handful of M&M's from the fridge. I showed him how the trick worked and we sat and practiced the special effects, over and over.

"Make the *whoosh* sound with your mouth before you suck in the M&M, then JUMP a little bit like it popped out of your butt!" He laughed when I said *Butt*.

"Okay . . . . I think you have it now! Show me from the beginning!"

He looked across the room at Lisa to distract my attention, and then he snuck an M&M under his leg. He looked now *at me* as he showed me the yellow M&M in his hand. "WHOOSH! . . . . OH!" with a jump . . . and eyes of surprise! And he reached down and produced the orange M&M from his . . . butt, and showed me.

"EXCELLENT!" I shook his hand and he smiled from ear to ear!

"BUTT!!!" We both giggled . . . "Didn't a yellow M&M go in your mouth?"

"Oops!"

We laughed some more.

Just tell them you are special. Not only can you fart an M&M but YOU ... can make it change colors!" as I looked at Lisa again shaking her head at me.

"Okay ... I think we are done!"

I moved onto the floor between Lisa's legs.

I laid my head back and she ran her fingers through my hair.

"I think I am going to drive in to the marina and see what's new down there. Would you like to go with me?" I asked.

"No ... I think I'm going to kid-nap your student, and take a nap."

*   *   *

I left in the rental car and started driving toward the marina. I took my time as I drove enjoying the large mahogany tree branches that came out over the road. I swung out into the other lane to give an old man on a bicycle extra space. He had his basket full of grocery bags and even had them hanging across his handlebars. Up ahead I saw the big sign of the Avis Car Rental Company where Loren works. I pulled off across the street into a bus stop area, and watched through the glass to see if I could see her. I missed her impulsiveness. I remembered the day in my bedroom while Lisa was here in Costa Rica.

"Can't hurt just to look." I said to the steering wheel.

She ran back and forth entering information on two different computers. She seemed to be really busy. Her blue one piece cotton uniform showed off her figure nicely.

I pulled out onto the pavement and continued toward the marina. It was a busy day in Limon, and it took longer than usual to get through town. I did not mind. For the last few years I have been rushing and in a hurry all the time. It felt good to have no urgent obligations.

I walked into the marina office and was immediately greeted by the manager.

"Mr. Bradford! I didn't see your vessel?"

"Oh . . . I'm not sailing on this trip. We flew in to stay with the Saborio's while we are having some work done on our house in Florida." I explained.

"It must be nice!" He said . . . "What can I do for you today?"

"I just needed something to do. Can you use any free labor today?" I asked.

"Hosea is over on C dock replacing some rotted wood on the inside of that old Pearson Sloop. He could probably use a second hand!"

"Cool! I'm headed that direction!" I was anxious to get to work.

I found Hosea up to his waist in cushions and access panels. He was not having a good day. His tools kept slipping and sliding down under the floorboards. It was very hot in the cabin and Hosea was covered in sweat as his clothes stuck to his body.

I went down into the cabin and watched what Hosea was doing. As I saw him getting ready to install a replacement piece, I found the 3M-5400 adhesive, and handed it to him. He squeezed it on the bottom of the piece and smashed it in place. He handed me back the caulking gun. I handed him a battery drill and the first screw.

"Thanks Capt.! My job is getting easier!" I finally saw a smile.

I picked up the piece that he would be doing next, and found some sandpaper on the countertop. I took it up on deck to sand it smooth as the wind blew the sawdust across the water.

I predrilled four holes with a corded drill and even countersunk the surface with a half-inch drill bit. I went back below deck and handed the piece to Hosea as he stood with the 5400 ready to go.

We worked for the next few hours putting the boat back together and cleaning up the debris from the repairs. I walked up to the office and bought two cold beers out of the soda machine. I handed one to Hosea as he put the last cushion back in place. We carried our beers up on deck and sat in the shade of the Bimini discussing how professionally we just completed this repair.

I was as sweaty as Hosea now and decided that I had successfully diverted enough boredom for one day.

I drove back to the house and parked the car by the front door. They were all sitting in front of the TV. I just waved as I passed through and headed for the shower. After my shower, I put on fresh clothes and decided to grab a quick nap.

When I woke up Loren and Andres had arrived to pick up David. Everyone was in the kitchen talking, while momma prepared another dinner for her family. I walked into the kitchen, greeted everyone with a smile, and then worked my way out the front door. The setting sun was blowing a cool breeze across the porch, and the house was hot from all the cooking.

Momma announced that the food was ready and for everybody to fill their own plate. There was a loud conversation in every room and I was in the mood for quiet. So ... after enough conversation to be cordial, I resumed my location on the front porch and continued picking at my food. I sat my empty plate on the handrail of the porch and started walking. I found myself retracing my steps to the channel as I took another sip of my beer. I stood on the creosote treated beams on the edge of the channel, staring into the moons reflection on the black water, remembering all the conversations that I had with David here.

In a lot of ways, I wish I had, had a child. If I could have had a clone of David that would probably all be fine, but kids do not come with a return policy and if I get the child from Hell . . . .

"Hi Jonah!" Said Loren, "I come here too when I need to think. So what are you doing here?" She asked.

"Thinking . . . ." as I smiled at her.

She walked over beside me and stood staring at my focal point in the water.

"So what do you see in there?" She asked.

"My own reflection . . . ." I was avoiding the truth.

"And what does that person in the reflection look like?"

I looked at her angrily as if she was forcing me to recognize an answer that I did not want to see.

"David and I came out here today and fished right here. We had a really good time and I could not believe how well we get along. He's a smart kid!" I looked back down into the water.

"He should be . . . he has a very intelligent father!" She said sweetly.

"Yes . . . you and Andres are great parents." I said.

I looked at Loren. She was shaking her head back and forth at me.

"You are so damned blind!" She said, as her attitude did a 180.

"Where did that come from?" I asked.

"Haven't you noticed that David's hair is a little bit light for a Costa Rican child?"

"Yes . . . but I thought maybe it would darken with age."

"No stupid . . . . have you noticed that he has flat feet?"

The color suddenly left my face. I stared at her and could not speak.

"Yes! . . . The answer to your question is yes!" She said.

"How?"

She giggled a little bit and stared me in the eyes.

"Well . . . other than the obvious answer . . . I have learned that Costa Rican birth-control pills don't work on Americans, evidently." She giggled a little bit more.

"I don't want anything from you, and I couldn't be happier that I have such a beautiful son. I just thought that it was time that you knew. Someday he will figure it out himself and *we* will have to deal with this. I just wanted you to have advance warning and time to think about how you will handle it." She said, as I stared into her watery eyes.

"HEY!!!!! There you are!!!"
As the entire dinner party had relocated to the canal.

Andres handed me another cold beer and took the empty bottle from my hand. He put his arm around Loren and looked into the water to see what she was looking at.

"David caught a big catfish right here today." I told Andres.

"Yeah he told me. He was so excited about it, and he also told me that he sent the big daddy catfish back to his family. That was cool!" Replied Andres.

Lisa came over and put her arm around me and looked up at me sensing that there was more going on than just reminiscing about catching a fish.

"He also showed us all how he could magically fart an M&M!" Said Lisa . . . and everyone broke out laughing.

I pointed at David, he was still laughing,

"You little tattletale!"

We all walked back to the house.

Chapter 9

The Jimenez family went back to their house and Lisa was soaking in a hot bathtub.

Momma Saborio came into the living room and sat down next to me on the couch.

We just stared at the TV, but we were not really watching it. She leaned her head over toward me and without taking her eyes off of the TV said;

"So now you know . . . Huh?"

I was shocked that she asked me that, and turned and stared her right in the eyes. I could tell this was a no bullshit moment and she was dead serious.

"Yes . . . Loren just told me tonight. Before tonight I didn't know." I confessed.

"How long have *you* known?" I asked.

"*Momma Saborio has always known.* I knew Loren was pregnant before she did. Mothers can tell these things!" She said proudly.

"Does Lisa know?" I asked.

"Not really . . . but you would be a stupid man to not think that she doesn't suspect it. Lisa will stay blind to this as long as someone does not force her to see it. She has never been a strong one for dealing with a tragedy. I will try to warn you if she starts asking me questions."

"Thanks." I kissed her on the forehead.

"Momma . . . What ever happened to *Poppa* Saborio?"

Her eyes went to her lap as she thought before speaking.

He was from Italy. He was a surveyor and had a job for the same Electric Company where Andres works. We met at a festival in town when I was much younger and prettier. We danced, and he kept coming back. That was ... 1945. We fell in love, got married, and in the first year had the girls. They sent him into the jungle in rainy season and he got malaria. Some people survive it ... Javani did not. I have taken care of the girls ... *all these years* ... by myself. This house was paid for by *my* parents, and I sewed to make money. My church friends helped sometimes too.

She became quiet and stayed with her memories a moment. She smiled, got up, and went to bed.

Lisa came out of the bathroom wearing a towel. She peaked around the corner into the living room, and wiggled her finger for me to follow her.

She tried to seduce me in the bedroom but the mattress was too squeaky, the walls were too thin, and in the end, I expressed a rare condition where *I was really not in the mood.*

I was waked up early by my cell phone ringing on the bedside table.

"Yello!" I said with my scratchy morning voice.

"Mr. Bradford! This is Jim with Orange Electric. We have got all the changes in your house done and we are here today waiting for the electrical inspector. What's my chance of getting a check from you guys?"

"Well Jim ... its 7 AM here in Costa Rica! Actually your chances of getting paid are pretty good" I took the phone and walked out onto the front porch.

"I can probably be back in Florida within the next two days and I can get you a check before your Friday payroll hits. Will that work for you?" I asked.

"That will be great! Just give me a call when you're ready and I'll pick it up there at your house."

"Okay Jim ... I'll see you soon!" .... *click!*

Lisa was ready to go home too. It was driving her crazy not being able to keep track of our stores and I think she was getting bored here. We went to work and booked flights to Florida for tomorrow morning. We even managed to get first-class seats.

* * *

We pulled into the garage and went into the house. We walked around inspecting and everything looked perfect. I went into the utility room, turned on the lights, and rejoiced loudly when I saw the bright orange occupancy permit stuck on the breaker panel.

"WE'RE LEGAL!!!!!! WE'RE LEGAL!!!!!! WE'RE LEGAL!!!!!! . . ." as I danced out onto the pool deck.

I called Orange Electric, and told him that the check was being written as we speak and that we would be here for the rest of the day if he wanted to pick it up.

We called the moving company and had them deliver our furniture from their storage facility the next day. The house in Brevard County had already been rented and was bringing in $1100 a month.

It took us several weeks to get all the boxes unpacked. Once the furniture and rugs were in place, and the cabinets and refrigerator fully stocked, it was starting to feel like home. Tonight would be the first night that we slept in the house. Lisa was in a real good mood. She kept sneaking up behind me and nibbling on my neck. Sometimes she would slide her hand across my buns as she walked past.

We decided to celebrate and go out to a very classy restaurant. Lisa wore a black sequined gown that she had designed. It was full length down to her heels, but was split up the left side almost to her hip. It overlapped just a bit so that you only got glimpses of her leg and never a complete view. She called it her *teaser gown*. What made it worse was that it had a full open back with two little black ties. She wore it with her black diamond earrings and her matching necklace that dangled a black diamond pendant between her breasts. She knew she was driving me crazy and teased me the entire evening. She occasionally slipped her foot out of her heel and checked my inseam under the table. She particularly liked to do it while the waiter was asking me a question.

On the way back to the house I reached across the console and pushed my hand into the cut on her dress. I slid my hand up higher and felt nothing but bare skin. I slid my hand forward as she separated her legs with her left leg now fully exposed. There was nothing but smooth skin between them.

"*You are such a bad girl!*" I said.

"*Only for you!*"

She smiled at me and laid her head back on the headrest.

It was a long drive back to the house and the foreplay came to a crescendo at the traffic light on SE St. Lucia Blvd.

Her seduction had now changed directions as my attention to the driving was a little bit neglected. She had unzipped my pants and was caressing my cock with both hands. I pulled the car into the garage and the door came down behind us. As I walked past the two other bays toward the house, the garage door opener light went out and I stopped. I could hear Lisa's heels clicking across the concrete floor coming toward me in the darkness. She kissed me, unfastened my belt, and pushed me backwards onto the hood of the Cherokee. Again she redirected my body's blood flow until she was satisfied with the line pressure. She pulled me up off of the hood and threw her body across it as she pulled her dress up with both hands exposing her beautifully shaped hips in the dim glow from the red, freezer light. I knew what to do from this point and I did it with . . . . enthusiasm. She jerked and moaned and suddenly reached back and grabbed my hips on both sides.

"STOP! Don't move!" She ordered and we both stood as manikins in the darkness.

I waited a few minutes, and started again.

"STOP!"

She stood up, took my hand, and pulled me down the hallway into the master bedroom. I pulled her gown off over her head and was again surprised to find absolutely nothing underneath. I became excited again and bent her across the bed. I continued stroking as I removed my tie, jacket, and shirt and then stepped out of my dress shoes and pants. She crawled up onto the bed and I followed her. She rolled over on her back with her head on the pillow. I pushed her legs against her chest and double-timed my pace. She beat my chest with her fists.

"STOP!" as she pulled out from under me and pushed me over onto my back.

She repositioned herself on top of me and slowly moved up and down. I was ready to explode any second. She had already been in a holding pattern for twenty minutes so I knew she was good to go.

"STOP!" I yelled *this time*. We were both hanging on the edge so close that the slightest movement would set us both off. She leaned forward and kissed me as I reached down and gently rubbed between her legs.

She looked at me in a panic mode, straightened up on me, and started jumping up and down as fast as she could. She screamed and giggled. I contorted and cramped. The electric shock shot through us strong enough to blow the main breaker on our new 300-amp service. We fell exhausted onto the king size mattress and just laid there for the longest time.

"Jonah! I want a baby!" She said most definitively.

"Well ... we can talk about that later, as I rolled over and started licking her nipples."

"Wait a minute .... are you still taking your birth control?" I asked.

"I quit taking them while we were in Costa Rica." She stared at my shocked face.

Suddenly my lower hydraulic pressure dropped to zero and I got out of the bed and took a shower.

Lisa was horny all the time now. She knew what to do to push my buttons, and did it at least . . . on a daily basis. Some of the following sexcapades were equally as intense as this past example. If she is ever going to get pregnant, I can pretty much guarantee that she already is.

She decided that to make this all more fun for me, that we should take a sailing vacation, and maybe go down to the Virgin Islands. Like I said, she knows how to push my buttons.

Two days later the house was in lockdown mode, and the Saborio was in route to the Virgin Islands. Sex on a sailboat, in the middle of a big empty ocean, with nothing to worry about but the big clear blue sky over your head, is the best place in the world to have sex. I adjusted the course and locked it into the autopilot as my beautiful naked wife took my hand and pulled me onto the forward deck.

The Saborio crashed through the swells and listed to starboard while the spray from the bow soaked our bodies and the deck. The water ran down the jib and created waves of water on the deck that splashed against our bodies and ran back along the cabin and jib sheets. The ocean action was so extreme that we had to lie sideways on the deck so I could brace my feet against the deck combing. When we both got close, Lisa rolled over onto her tummy and crawled higher across the deck until she could hang on to a stanchion post. She spread her legs as I mounted her from behind and brought it all to a salty and exciting conclusion.

We carefully moved back to the cockpit, trying to suppress scary thoughts of falling overboard completely naked. We laughed and hugged each other as I adjusted the sails and realized how dangerous sex on the front deck under sail is.

"That was great!" She said still breathing heavily.

"Yes it was!" I agreed, "Wanna do it again?"

She smacked me and went below.

*   *   *

We spent a few days on a transient dock in Puerto Rico. Lisa, of course, made the rounds of the clothing shops and found several new styles that she bought in her size to copy the design. The marina that we stayed at had free Wi-Fi access and as I signed into my e-mail account I saw that there were several e-mails from Loren in Costa Rica.

I waited for Lisa to get back to the boat before I opened them, and we sat at the galley table and read them together.

She said that Momma Saborio and David were doing fine and that she had been promoted to the assistant manager position at the Avis Rental Car Company. She said that David is learning to read already. She has to work really hard to keep him interested, because he thinks it is all too easy. He is a really smart kid. She bought him a model sailboat kit that was rated for kids 16 or over. David built it in two weeks and already has it displayed on the shelf in his bedroom.

She said that Andres and her have had a lot of problems. His job at CNFL has been keeping him away from home longer than usual. The last time they sent his crew out to install a new power line, he was gone for an entire month. He seems to like being with his crew more than being with his family. She says that they really enjoyed our visit with them, and to come back soon.

"I hate to hear that about Andres," Said Lisa, "they looked like they were doing so well."

"Yes .... but I know a lot of guys that have jobs on the road like that. They get lonely being so far away from home, and a lot of times cheat on their wife." I said.

"Well he better not cheat on my sister!" Said Lisa sternly.

We left Puerto Rico the next day and continued toward the US Virgin islands. We had been to St. Thomas before and decided to skip all of the tourist interaction and go directly to St. Croix.

We were lucky enough to find an open dock in Gallows Bay just east of Christiansted Harbor. I backed the Saborio into a dock and tied off. The harbormaster directed me to the customs office and told me to check in at the marina office when I was finished. We did as instructed and I paid for the dock at the lower *weekly* rate. We went back to the boat and got a change of clothes, towels, and the shampoo, and headed for the marina showers. On the boat, we have to be so careful about our water supply. It is really nice to be able to stand in a hot shower for a while

As Lisa stood in the jewelry store trying to make up her mind between black diamonds and black coral, I was looking at a few items on the other side of the store. They had an actual gold coin that was recovered from a shipwreck, complete with documentation and a photo, for what I felt was a very reasonable price. They also had a pendant that was made from Lorimar and set into a gold free-form bezel, with an antique 18K chain. They gave me a highly reduced price on my two items after they realized the amount of money that Lisa was about to spend. It was slow season in St. Croix and this jewelry store was very happy about our purchases.

"What did you buy, Jonah?" Asked Lisa.

"Gifts for Loren and David."

I took them from the bag and showed her.

"Oh! Loren will love this. They have never seen anything like this in Costa Rica!" as she picked up David's coin.

"Don't you think he's a little young for this, maybe?"

"Maybe right now .... but Loren can keep it for him until he is older. Gold prices are getting higher every day and something this antique in solid gold may help put him in college someday."

I put it back into the wooden box and then back into the bag with Loren's necklace.

* * *

Back on the boat, I admired the black coral earrings and pendant that Lisa bought and asked her to model them for me. She went into the head and put them on in the mirror and came back out.

"I don't know .... they don't do much for you in a Carlos Santana T-shirt." I smiled.

She flashed me a very sexy Costa Rican smile, disappeared into the master cabin, and shut the door. She came back out a few minutes later in a black silk nighty.

"Oh yes! That definitely goes perfect with black coral!"

She backed into the master cabin and I followed.

On our third day here in St. Croix, Lisa had become friends with the owner of a women's fashion shop. They obviously had a lot of things in common and they talked about their businesses and new fashions. *Gloria* invited Lisa to fly over to St. Thomas with her and attend an *invitation only* fashion tradeshow. Lisa was excited, but hated to leave me in St. Croix by myself. I convinced her to go with Gloria and I would hang around sailboat places that she normally did not like to go.

Sunrise the next morning, Gloria and Lisa boarded the seaplane. It roared as it lifted out of the water and grabbed air over the sailboat. It banked off to the North and I watched it disappear toward St. Thomas.

I went back to bed and slept until the heat in the boat sent me ashore. I ran into an auction over on Company Street and although there were a lot of very good deals, I did not buy anything! The things that I liked were too big to fit in the sailboat, or too big to send airfreight. I walked through the archways and the worn terraced sidewalks of King Street. I turned near the Post Office, and noticed a little bar in an alley off of the boardwalk. I walked inside and went back into a quiet corner. I sat at a small round table where I could see everyone in the bar, and all of the tourist outside.

"Hi my name is Nastasya; I will be your server! Can I get you something cold to drink?"

I sat hypnotized staring into her cobalt blue eyes framed with her long dark hair. She also carried a fairly noticeable baby bump.

"Sir?"

"Oh yes . . . . do you have Killian's Red on tap?"

"Yes we do, I will be right back!" I admired her long hair as she walked away.

She sat my chilled glass, and a bottle of Killian's, on coasters. She laid down a menu, and I leafed through it trying to make up my mind.

"The chef here makes a killer stuffed yellow tail!" Suggested Nastasya.

"That sounds good! Make it so!" We exchanged smiles.

I finished my meal, and sat my empty glass on a five-dollar tip.

Nastasya came back to the table as I was standing. She pulled the five dollars out from under the glass and thanked me for it. She had changed clothes and was wearing cut off Levi's and a loose T-shirt.

"Are you off now?" I asked.

"Yes, I have to go over to the airboat dock and pick up a friend." She said.

"My wife is coming in on that flight too!"

"Well come on . . . . you can ride with me!" She took my hand and pulled me out of the bar.

"Do you live here year round?" I asked as she drove.

"Yes, I have a big house on top of a mountain, out on the East end."

"Woooo!!! Must be nice!" I looked her over again.

She laughed . . . . "I just *house sit* it! You know where I work!" She continued laughing.

We stood together as the plane landed and roared up onto the ramp. I saw Lisa and Gloria coming down the stairway, waved goodbye to Nastasya, and thanked her for the ride. A young man in a white shirt carrying a small black dog came down the stairway as Nastasya smiled and hugged him.

We walked with Gloria to the car lot and she dropped Lisa and me off at the marina.

As we sat on the boat watching the sunset behind the smoke over the power plant, Lisa got sort of moody.

"Gloria got me an appointment with her female gynecologist tomorrow." She smiled at me.

"So . . . are you pregnant?" I asked.

"I think so!" She got all excited, "We will know for sure tomorrow!"

Chapter 10

"I'M GOING TO BE A MOMMY!"

L isa was so excited I thought she was going to explode. She danced her way down the dock and onto the boat. She grabbed me and kissed me as she touched down in the cockpit.

"You're going to be a daddy!" She said and waited for my reaction.

I put on my best smile and hugged her tightly so she could not see any further lack of excitement. My sisters had kids and I know what comes next. I felt like life as I know it, was about to end. My on demand sailing, and spontaneous sex, was about to be preempted by a 24-hour a day observer that cries with an 18 year *plus* payment plan.

I faked another excited smile and went back to the galley table where my laptop computer was still on. As I sat and stared at the screen I thought about writing another book about the transition that I am about to experience. I am sure that I am not the only one that is going to have to go through this. I had a few ideas about how to start the book and filed them in my memory until after I check my e-mail.

We had several e-mails from various store locations that were requesting advice on a problem or additional inventory.

"NEXT ....NEXT ....DELETE ....NEXT ....JimenezOne .... OPEN!"

Lisa and Jonah,

Hope you are having fun in the Virgin Islands. I wish I was with you. It has done nothing but rain here for the past three weeks.

Thanks for the gifts. I wear my Lorimar all the time and everyone asked me what it is. David wants to see his coin every few days, which his uncle Jonah bought him, but I keep it locked up in my jewelry box until he is older. Momma is still momma, and for her age she is still looking good and staying very healthy. She asked me about you two often and misses you a lot.

Now for the bad news! Andres has not come home in almost two months now. He used to send checks when he was gone for a long time, but now the checks have quit coming too. A couple weeks ago I found a charge to our credit card for a car repair. I went through the Avis computer and checked out the invoice on the car. It was registered to a Maria Gomez in Cortez. I got our company attorney to follow up on it and he informed me that Andres had been supporting a woman in Cortez for many years now and had three children by her. Evidently a lot of the time that I thought he was working on overhead lines, he was burying cable.

My first impulse was to try to work things out with him, but with three kids and another woman I don't know how that would be possible. The company attorney recommended a good local divorce attorney that I have an appointment with tomorrow. I will keep you informed with all of this happy news.

David says to tell you to not let Lisa drive . . . . kerplunk!!! Whatever that means??

Love you both!!
Loren

Of course Lisa wanted to *immediately* e-mail her back and give her the news about being pregnant. Lisa typed faster than I did so I turned her loose on my laptop and let her send the 10-page e-mail to Loren.

It made me very happy to see Lisa so excited but I was having trouble reciprocating.

The vacation had achieved the purpose that Lisa designed it for, and she was anxious now to get back to our home and prepare for the child. We took a leisurely sail through the Bahamas and reduced the night crossings as much as we could. We tried to drop the hook on a different island by sunset, every day. As we started the final crossing back to the St. Lucie Inlet, Lisa came up on deck wearing a thin white T-shirt and white bikini bottoms. She walked around the wheel and climbed onto my lap facing me. I smiled at her and she stared into my eyes.

"I love you Jonah." She whispered.

"I love you too, Lisa" I smiled and started pushing her T-shirt up her waste.

She smiled back at me and raised her arms over her head. I threw her T-shirt into the cockpit floor then pulled the strings on both sides of her bikini bottoms. I was wearing thin nylon swim trunks that easily pulled up above my inflating member. Lisa took care of the alignment.

"I love sex on the ocean!" . . . . Evidently Lisa does too.

*　　*　　*

Shortly after we got home, she hired a fashion designer to work directly between her and the manufacturer in Costa Rica. She gave *Georgia* a generous expense account and suggestions on where to travel to get new ideas for the *Saborio Line*.

A lot of the intimate apparel designs were actually from me. Whenever I ran into situations where some part of the lingerie caused an interruption in the male testosterone, I would reconfigure that problem to become more enticing and less of a distraction. Lisa loved it when I did this but still claimed it as her own ideas to the employees.

I could not help but have my future child on my mind, I also often thought of my pre-existing son in Costa Rica. If she ended up divorced from Andres, her income would be so low that she would probably have to leave her house and move back in with momma. When both of the girls lived there, they helped momma pay the bills, and right now I did not know how she was even getting by.

I called Momma Saborio one day while Lisa was touring the shops. She told me that Loren had filed for divorce. Andres was showing such a low income, that he had to get a public defender, and didn't even want the house since there was still a loan on it. He was agreeable to a peaceful divorce, and at this point they were only going through the waiting period and the signatures. She also told me that Andres had always known that David was not his son, so there were no custody issues either.

I told momma to go to her bank and set up a new checking account for her and Loren jointly. I told her that after she gets it set up to call me, and give me the bank account number. I will start regularly making deposits from Florida to help with whatever expenses may come up.

Momma called me on my cell phone about three weeks later while I was sitting at the galley table of the sailboat. She told me that Loren's divorce was final and Loren had sold the house and made enough money to pay it off and have a little extra. She put the proceeds into the new checking account, and then momma gave me the account number so I could do bank transfers. She thanked me and begged me to come and visit David.

As soon as I closed my cell phone I went back online and set up an automatic transfer into her account for $1000 American / $1,012,000 Colones on the first of every month.

Lisa was starting to show now and paraded it around the house proudly. She was still impulsive and a bit more emotional, and the pregnant thing is not as tough as I expected.

One day while I sat below deck typing into my laptop computer. I heard Lisa's flip-flops coming across the pool deck and out onto the dock. I watched as she came down the companionway steps and slid in beside me at the galley table.

Her eyes were all watery and at first I thought there was a problem with the baby. She turned me toward her and scooted in against me in order to hug me tightly. She squeezed me for a long time with her head almost against my back. She readjusted her position and planted her head against my chest.

"Jonah . . . . I am so very happy! I just felt like I had to tell you that, and thank you for making my life complete. You took me away from a poverty situation and gave me the world!" as the tears started running down her face.

I hugged her tightly until I saw the smile return to her face.

"I've got a pot of coffee brewing right now. Would you like me to bring you a cup?" She asked

"That would be perfect!"

I watched her climb the stairway and *flip-flop* back into the house.

When she returned, my fingers were flying on the keyboard. She has learned to not interrupt me until the fingers stop. She sat the coffee on the galley table and smiled at me as she exited again without saying a word.

The smell of amaretto filled the boat.
I finished my thought, and took a sip of the *Amaretto with Coffee.*

My publisher actually showed up at our house with a photographer and said that he wanted some pictures of me working on the book. He loves the idea that my office was actually a sailboat and had the photographer take several transitional pictures between the house and my floating office.

"It fits your stories Jonah! I couldn't have *written* it any better!" and he laughed.

"So can I read the manuscript that you are working on now?" He asked.

"NO . . . . This one is a little different than my normal books. It will be about five more months before I have it completed!" I put my hand on Lisa's tummy.

He smiled at her and laid another check on the table.

Lisa spoke with the doctor on the phone, and he offered to do an ultrasound to learn the sex of the baby. We deliberated over the answer and decided that we DO want to know! I drove Lisa to the doctor's office and was able to see my baby on a TV monitor.

"It's a boy!" Said the doctor.

"YES!" I swung my fist through the air.

Lisa and I would've been perfectly happy with a daughter, but down deep we were both more excited that it was a boy.

Now Lisa had a color scheme to go with, and I was excited that it was not pink. I inadvertently was making future plans for things to do with my son, and occasionally drifting off thinking about David in Costa Rica, wishing I could spend more time with him.

We decided that we were still far enough out, that it was probably safe to make a quick visit to Costa Rica and flaunt Lisa's big belly to the family. She was still getting up and down the stairways with little effort, but it was a little more involved getting her into an airplane seat. Each time that we changed planes I studied the passengers trying to guess which one was a doctor, just in case.

Loren and David picked us up at the airport in Limon, and once we got back to momma's house the women all divided off in the one room. They carried on loud and giggly conversations in a woman's language that David and I did not understand. In a way that worked out good, because for the next few days David and I spent almost all of our time together. I am going to have a hard time leaving him when it is time to go home. I was curious about my unborn son's appearance. Since the mothers are twins and I am the father of both boys, my *new* son should look very similar to David? All kinds of crazy thoughts were running through my mind including ducking out someplace with Loren and her nice tight body. It was hard for me to imagine that Loren had to have looked like Lisa at some point and managed to tighten it all back up.

"What are you staring at?" Asked Loren from the kitchen.

"I am just fascinated with all the variations of the female body!" She wiggled her butt at me and smiled over her shoulder. I blushed and the entire kitchen crew laughed at me. David saved me as he dropped a magazine onto my lap and started telling me about a boat that he liked.

We flew back to Florida and finished the details on **Daniel's room**. We heard the name on the plane and we both agreed that we liked it. Lisa concentrated on furniture, toys and necessities, while I installed baby monitors and a separate temperature control.

We slowed down our life style and it worried me to even watch her go to the grocery. She would carry in half of the bags before asking me to help. She swam in the pool every evening and for a woman that was almost ready to pop, she was not showing much fat on her body. She called Loren about twice a week just to be sure that *"Things were supposed to feel like this?"*

Although Lisa's sex drive had dropped to ... *almost gone* .... mine seemed to go the other way. I was horney all the time and it wasn't from looking at my wife's sexy body. It must have been pheromones! Even though she occasionally offered a less invasive solution, it was too few and far between. I fantasized about Loren in Costa Rica, Annie over at the marina, Zuri in the Bahamas, and the Papa John's pizza delivery girl!

"I'm never going to survive this! AAAaahhhhh!!!!"

A few weeks later I was sitting in the sailboat typing away on the laptop and my cell phone started ringing.

"Jonah!!!!! Jonahhhh!"

"Yes Lisa ... Where are you?" I asked.

"I'm in the house .... It's time! .... the contractions are getting worse! AAaahh!" She said as another one hit.

I was already running toward the house while we continued talking on the cell.

When I reached the house, she was standing by the door to the garage with a travel bag in hand.

"Are we good to go?" I asked.

"Yes." and she hung on to me.

I walked her to the Cherokee and ran the seat belt above her bump. I ran around the car and hit the garage door opener as I started the car and backed out onto the pavers.

She stayed calm all the way and I rolled her into the emergency ward with a little class.

Evidently we were too composed, because everyone ignored us. "I HAVE A PREGNANT WOMAN HERE!!!!! SHE'S GOING TO HAVE A BABY ANY SECOND!!!" I screamed.

Suddenly I had three nurses and a doctor all over her and I was being told to go sign her in. When I told them . . . "*Screw that!!*" and tried to go through the doors with her, two orderlies grabbed my arms and delivered me to the registration window.

The contractions were increasing before I got the paperwork filled out, and they took me right to her and asked if I was the coach.

We had practiced that, so I said, "*Yes!*" and started doing my thing.

This was my first . . . delivery. I didn't let it show . . . . but I was nervous. I had several, *three second*, flashbacks of things that I had told my friends over the years.

"*Oh hell no!* I don't want kids. I love my life style"

"Married . . . . *Oh hell no!* Do you expect me to keep sleeping with the *SAME* woman?

I would go insane! Do I look like a *mini-van Daddy* to you? Ha . . . Ha!"

"KIDS!!!! *Oh hell no!* I'd have to sell my sailboat! You KNOW, that's not going to happen."

An hour later . . . . *or maybe three hours later* . . . . I was introduced to;

> *Daniel Michael Bradford . . .*
> *The future heir to my throne!*

Chapter 11

I was a little disappointed. All he did was poop, cry, and suck on Lisa's breasts. Lisa never had big breasts and now that she developed some girth, it is all for the baby. I tried not to be jealous but I had been used to getting all the attention, and now I was the secondary human.

Lisa had her bad days too, now that she was *mommy* . . . 24 hours a day. Daniel seemed to wake up and scream every three to five hours, and both of us had aged twenty years in the last two months.

"I never want to have sex again!" I decided. "If I can get through this one I will get a vasectomy!"

I needed some ocean time so bad I couldn't stand it, but that was not on the agenda for a few more years now.

I considered hiring some outside help to keep up with Daniel. I could swear that there was more coming out then I was feeding in! Suddenly I had a *revelation!*

Momma Saborio would probably love to come and see her second grandson. I talked it over with Lisa and she agreed and made the phone call. A week later I picked momma up at OIA and had her room already prepared in the house. Daniel liked her instantly. Momma told us that our only problem was that Daniel was picking up on how nervous and insecure we both were.

"No new parent knows all the rules when they start. When you first developed an interest in sailing, we're you as experienced as you are now?" She ask.

"I've got your point . . . . Thanks."

I thought about the image we projected to the kid. A few weeks later momma returned to Costa Rica and turned her efforts to helping Loren.

* * *

Things eventually smoothed out and Lisa and I actually started enjoying being parents. As her body got back into form, so did our impulsive sex life, and I personally made sure that the birth control pills were current. Sometimes, as I played with Daniel, I had fleeting thoughts of switching them for Extasy, but got a grip and let it be. Daniel had naptime every day after lunch and the adults had grown-up time, two doors down the hall.

Much to my surprise, life was returning to . . . *my* . . . normal, and I discovered that you can basically take a baby anyplace that I went before. He drew a myriad of attention in the bar as I sat and had a coffee. When Lisa headed for the shop, it was just Daniel and me, and I was getting pretty good at it. It helped that Daniel was such an easy kid. He even slept in the V-berth while I typed in the main cabin. I think the ticking away of my laptop became a soothing sound to him. As long as I typed he stayed asleep. *Most of the time!*

Sometimes when I write . . . I read aloud what I typed to see how it flows. One day while I was typing and Daniel was asleep in the V-berth, I heard him repeating some of the words that I spoke. I continued, and although he skipped or distorted some of the complicated words. He put together chopped up sentences from copying me. I could not get him to do it for Lisa.

* * *

The Connie Miller, "Just for Girls", talk show, had called Lisa a few weeks ago and had a short notice slot, that she needed to fill. Lisa accepted immediately and saw it as free advertising. The host was interested in her story and asked her if she minded getting into her Costa Rican / American transition. She agreed and they scheduled her on the show.

"Today we have the creator of the Saborio Fashions Empire. She has come from a small hourly job in Costa Rica and spread her clothing line around the world. Please welcome Lisa Saborio Bradford!"

Music played as Lisa strutted her newest design across the stage and sat beside the host.

"Look Daniel . . . That's mommy on TV."

"Mommy." He pointed at the big screen.

"Lisa. How did you go from working as a clerk in a fashion store, to becoming the wealthiest female entrepreneur in the United States?"

"Well actually . . . It was the idea of my husband, Jonah Bradford."

"Jonah Bradford the Author?"

"Yes. He presented the idea to me in a traffic jam in Limon. I thought he was breaking up with me and I fought with him loudly outside of the car. I didn't realize at the time, that he was proposing a lifelong business arrangement between us"

"That is so romantic. Lisa . . . look at the screen behind you."

"OOOooo!" from the audience.

"That's my son . . . Daniel."

"Daniel . . . Where is Daniel today?" asked Connie.

"He is watching this at home in Florida, with his father."

She did her Carol Burnett finger wiggle at the camera, as Jonah and Daniel did it back to the TV.

"Do you miss Costa Rica?"

"Not Costa Rica as much as my family."

"That would be Maria Saborio, and your TWIN SISTER, Loren?"

Another photo flashed on the studio screen.

"Yes Loren was here a while and went back." Lisa said sadly.

"Well Lisa . . . Tell us a little bit about your business."

"We started with just the one shop in Orlando, added another one in Viera, and then mortgaged everything we have to expand. It kept growing beyond what we could control, so we sold franchises."

"So where do you get these ideas for your beautiful designs?"

The TV showed a fashion show with the Saborio models showcased.

"We own a beautiful sailboat. We travel all over and see styles from all over the world. We monitor the corporation with satellite communications on the boat. Jonah even has it set up to monitor the cash flow and receive a live video feed from our stores. Being an author, he can write *anyplace*, and then email his manuscript to the publisher."

"Okay, Lisa. We have to go to a commercial break and afterwards we will be joined by Jenny O'Dell, singing her latest hit ... *Break me-Shake me*"

"Daniel ... Time for you to go to bed. Mommy is all done." I said.

RRRrrring ... RRRrrring!

"Yello! Yes! we were watching.... Yes ... you looked beautiful! ... Unhh Huh! Make the taxi driver go slow to the hotel and we will see you tomorrow afternoon ... Love you too ... Bye."

"Well Daniel ... Mommy is very excited. Why don't we eat some pasticcio ice cream before we go to bed?"

* * *

Lisa was going to be home all week and I was curious what had grown on the bottom of the Saborio. I motored the boat up to the marina where I had an appointment for the boat to be hauled. I stayed with her until she was blocked up, tucked away, and the yacht lift had returned to the dock. The bottom looked like a wet green shag carpet and I hired two of the yard boys to blow it off with a pressure sprayer before it dried. She looked considerably happier now and I handed each man two twenties. I walked over to the yard office, signed the papers, and ask if anyone was going my way in the next few hours. There were still a few things I could go do on my boat if I had to wait.

They joked that no one that works here could get past the gate in my neighborhood. I called Lisa and asked her to come and get me when she had time. I told her where the boat was located and went back to cleaning.

I walked through the ship yard detouring past all of the big commercial boats that tie up on the pier. I admired these giant sea monsters and the unusual names given them.

"*Uncle Tom*" . . . . ? "*Uncle Tom* . . . ?" That sounds familiar as I stepped back and looked it over.

Two men were standing on deck looking at me . . . looking at their ship.

I waved and continued back into the yard.

Lisa picked me up at our boat, with Daniel in a child's seat in the back. I got into the passenger seat, and spotted the two men standing beside another boat, taking a cell phone picture of us driving away. They walked toward the *Saborio* and took another photo of the *name* on the transom.

"Oh shit! I know who they are!" I said, not realizing I was speaking out loud.

"Who . . . who is it?" Lisa asked.

"Drive! . . . . Just drive!" I said hastily.

On the way home I told Lisa that those were two men from the *Uncle Tom*. Her memory popped back into place and her hands were shaking on the steering wheel. We went into the house and thought things through. I called our company attorney and had him check the status of the trafficking charges that were brought against Captain Raymond. I knew he was supposed to be in prison but it sure looked like someone was doing business with his freighter.

Our attorney called us back a few hours later and told us that Raymond had been released early due to lack of cell space in the prison.

"Just chock another one up to Governor Scotty!" He said.

"Okay thanks." and I hung up the phone.

"Well . . . He knows we are here, and he knows where our boat is. He has probably also figured out that his money paid for it. If we go to the boat he will have us followed or captured. If we move the boat he will have us followed. I guess for now we just leave the boat alone and watch for him to go to sea." I rationalized.

"Sounds like a plan." Said Lisa, "Do you think he will go to Costa Rica?"

"I doubt it! *You* are the primary one he wants!" I said reluctantly.

I held her in my arms all night. She was very scared and so was I. I controlled my considerations and made love to her gently for hours. I transported her to a happier place. After we finished, she was tired ... *I was exhausted* ... and we slept uninterrupted for the rest of the evening.

*   *   *

In the morning I was staring into my coffee, when Lisa looked at me across the table.

"What are you thinking about?" She asked.

"I'm thinking that as long as he is here, you and Daniel may be safer with your family in Costa Rica. We're too close here!" I said seriously.

"She nodded her head in agreement."

"You should come too!" She said.

"No ... I want to keep an eye on him. Maybe I can get him arrested again, and now that he has a prison history ... maybe they can give him life!" I said with a false smile.

She nodded her head again ....."I'll book reservations."

"NO! He is probably monitoring the commercial airlines. I know a man that works for Caribbean Air. It is a small airline, thirty people per plane maximum. Most people aren't aware of it. Let me call him!"

I looked up his number and walked out on the deck.

He says he can do it, but he wants to have all your documentation the day before so he can process it himself. You will leave the US with one name, and arrive in Costa Rica with your real passport and name. The switch will happen at your transfer. He is bending a few rules with the witness protection regulations.

He can get you out of here tomorrow morning, if I can take him all your documentation before the end of his shift today.

"When is the end of his shift?" Lisa asked.

I looked at my watch . . . "Two hours! Get me your passport and I'll change clothes real quick."

She brought me down her passport, and Daniels birth certificate. I jumped into my truck and headed for a small airport near Palm City. I arrived at the airport and Paul was waiting for me.

"Thanks for staying over! I got here as fast as I could!" I said.

"No problem . . . You got her passport and the baby's birth certificate?" Ask Paul.

"Yes! It's inside her passport."

He stood looking at everything.

"Okay ! Let me go see what I can do?" and he started walking away.

"Paul!"

"Yeah!"

"You might need this too!"

I reached out and put ten folded fifty dollar bills into his hand.

"Wow! Thanks Jonah!"

He started to pull away and I held onto his hand.

"Just take care of my family!"

After a serious stare . . . . I released him.

He gave me the *thumbs up*, and then trotted down the hallway.

"I had done all that I can for now, but I kept going over it and over it as I drove back to Port Saint Lucie. I got off on Rt.76 N and thought that I would go by the marina on the way and talk to the men in the office. I turned right at the light and down the hill and another quick right into the marina. I drove to the far end, parking across from the marina bar, and then went into the office.

"Hey Rick! I am Jonah Bradford. I have the Hylas 46 over in the back row." I announced.

"I know who you are Mr. Bradford! What can I do for you?" Came a response from the big man behind the front desk. He wore white shorts and a flowered shirt.

I pointed to his back office. He stood up, led me into it, closing the door behind us.

"I've had some bad history with one of your other patrons here, and I just wanted to be sure they haven't been inquiring about me?"

"So who would that be, Mr. Bradford?" as he pulled out his ledger book.

"*Uncle Tom,* over on the pier."

Rick closed his ledger book.

"Bradford . . . You're messing with some bad actors over there dude." He said sincerely.

"Let me talk to my men. They'll be in here to get their checks in about 5 minutes."

He left me in the office and brought me a cold Pepsi while I waited.

He came back in two or three minutes.

"Tommy tells me that they came in here and got the address of your home from the name on the back of the boat. They told him that the two of you had some business that needed finished." Rick said somberly.

"So they gave them my *HOME* address?" I yelled!

"I guess so." Said Rick.

I busted out of the door and ran to my truck. I broke all speed limits while I tried to call Lisa on the cell phone.

It kept kicking me over to her voice mail, which has been a problem in this house because of all the new overhead lighting.

I pushed the red traffic light like a true Floridian. I pulled into the driveway and shut off the truck at the front door. The door was unlocked and as I went inside, I heard Daniel crying from his room.

"LISA!.... LISA!...." I ran down the hall and into our room. The bedspread was out of place and Lisa's robe and clothes were laid on the dresser. I walked into the master bath slowly watching for anyone else that may still be in the house. I looked through the door and froze in my tracks.

"LISA!!!!!!!! NOOOOOOOOOOOOOOOO!!!!!"
I reached into the bathtub water and raised her head. I drug her wet body onto the ceramic tile floor as water ran out into the bedroom. I tried CPR until I almost passed out.
"BREATHE DAM IT!!!!!! BREATHE!!!!!!!!!!!" I finally gave up and cried on her stomach. I stood and looked at her, as she laid pale and wet in my favorite black nighty. She must have been planning a big night for me before she flew back to Costa Rica.

"911 ... What is your emergency?"

Chapter 12

"Mr. Bradford, do you have any idea who might have done this to your wife?" The Detective asks.

"**No** . . . . My wife didn't have any enemies."

"Where were you between 4 and 6 PM?"

"I was driving back from Palm City. If you check my truck the dam motor is probably still warm." I answered bitterly.

"Do you have someone who can collaborate your story?"

"Sure."

I pulled up Paul's phone number, hit send, and handed it to the detective.

"Hello Sir, I am Detective O'Malley. I am a Martin County Homicide Detective. I have a . . . Mr. Bradford with me right now who claims he was with you earlier this evening. Can you tell me what time he was last within eye contact of you?"

"Yeah . . . sure . . . Is Jonah Okay?" Paul asked.

"Just answer the question, Sir!" The detective asks sternly.

"Well . . . he got here about 3:30 or 4:00 and he left about 4:00 to 4:30. He should have got home about 5:00 to 5:30! Can I talk to Jonah?" Paul asks.

"Later!" . . . *click!*

"Okay Mr. Bradford. I'm sorry we had to do that but the husband is ALWAYS our first suspect. Here's my card and *don't leave town!*" The detective ordered.

They put Lisa's body in the ambulance and quietly left the neighborhood. I was numb! There were not any feelings! Just the image of her wet cold body sticking against the back of my eyes. I visualized Captain Raymond holding her head below the water as she fought for her final breath. I wanted to kill . . . . and right now there was enough controlled energy in my body to burn a path from here to California. I walked into Daniels room and calmly thanked the police officer for taking care of him. I carried him into the kitchen and got his supper ready on the stove. The policewoman now re-assured that I wasn't going to go crazy, gave me another card and told me to call her if I needed help with Daniel. She could provide me with some recommendations. I glanced at her card, thanked her, and shut the door behind her.

I kept most of the house lights off because I figured the Uncle Tom boys would be watching me now. I pulled all the curtains and I noticed an undercover car parked down the street.

"They need to start buying hub caps! Don't they Daniel?"

"Hub caps . . . he, he, he!"

The little turd forced a smile out of me.

He had no idea of the evil that his Daddy was planning. I figure my phones were bugged, so I called a babysitter that we had used. I asked her if she could come over for a little while. I told her that I had to do some writing in the boat and that Lisa was gone tonight. She showed up a half hour later and we checked in on Daniel.

"Julie . . . . I will give you $20.00 to let me use your cell phone for a few minutes. Mine is broken!"

"Sure Mr. Bradford!" I laid the twenty in her hand. I took the phone and walked out toward the dock while she turned on the TV.

"RRrrrring . . . RRRRrring . . . You dialed the number, you know who I am. Leave a message and if I like it I may call you back!" *BEEP!*

"DISCO SUCKS 248-555-5555!" . . . *CLICK!*

And I waited . . . .

"RRrring . . . . Yello!"

"Jonah! My old bud . . . What can I do ya for?"

123

When I heard his scratchy voice again, I relaxed knowing that we were about to *create* closure. At the same time, I shook in my flip-flops as I realized that we were about to murder a . . . *human* . . . and were going up against some very nasty men.

I spent the next few minutes telling him the story of Uncle Tom, and Lisa. He was shocked that I *finally* got married. He asked me several questions and I knew all the right answers and details.

"Well Jonah . . . I have a new creation here that I have never used before. This sounds like the ideal situation to do a test run. Can you get me an Airline ticket from Michigan to someplace close?" Michigan asked.

"Yeah! I'll book you into the Palm City Airport."

"Okay and I will need a local hotel room that I can build the new toy in. I can't move this product on an airline . . . . *fucking Homeland Security* . . . you know." Michigan replied.

"Got you covered! I know what you like to carry. I will slip it into the rental car for you."

As long as I have known Michigan, he has always loved his 44 Magnum. Even when he went by his . . . *real* . . . name, he always traveled with an arsenal. When he was younger I taught him to play guitar. As payment for my lessons, he took me out one night and had me assist him in a mock ambush of a white Volkswagen. We ran invisible trip lines across a bridge and had simulators on each side. We drove his Gremlin up on a nearby hill and parked in a church parking lot. We got two Michelobs out of the cooler. The bug was on schedule as Michigan stepped out into the cold night air.

BOOM . . . BOOM!!! and the VW screeched to a stop fifty yards after the bridge.

The red smoke billowed from both canisters and the white car's paint was turned to pink. Michigan's adrenalin was peaked. He yelled, swung his fists, and was excited like a football fan at the Super Bowl. I realized then, that I was seeing a career move. He scared me when he got like this, but he came back to reality after I grabbed his shoulders and jolted him back. He would have killed anyone else. *We were seventeen years old.*

"Deal!" Said Michigan, "Leave the itinerary on my answering machine . . . time is up! Bye!" The call was terminated.

I went back into the house and handed the cell phone to Julie. I handed her another twenty-dollar bill and told her it was a long distance call.

"That should more than cover it. Are you available tomorrow?" I ask her.

"All day?" she asked.

"Maybe?" I waited for an answer.

"Call me when you're ready!" She waved the bills at me and went out of the door.

Daniel was asleep for the night, so I poured a double Rum & Coke and sat in front of the TV.

The next morning I called the baby sitter, drove to the airport, and called Paul on an internal airport phone. He came out into the hallway to meet me. I gave him the name and times for Michigan, and explained to him what happened to Lisa. I wanted Paul to make the reservations for the flight and the rental car. He felt terrible about Lisa and left me in a break room while he went to the main office. He returned with Lisa's passport and sadly put it into my hand.

"Inside the passport is a printout of Michigan's itinerary and a reservation for a particular rental car, reserved for business executives. Your son's birth certificate is also inside. Is there anything else I can do for you?" Asked Paul

"No . . . Thank you."

I put the passport in my side pocked and left the building.

*   *   *

I went from the airport, to a large flea market and found a man that was always dealing guns. He was always priced to high so we had never made a successful deal. Today was his lucky day. He had a Mossberg 12 Ga. Pump and a 44 Magnum still in the display box. He made me a group price of $1700. I told him we had a deal, and started pulling off hundred dollar bills.

"Wait, Buddy! . . . I am a Federal Firearms Dealer. There is a 30-day hold and a background check first. I crammed the money back in my pocket and walked away.

"Hey! HEY!! Don't go away so fast! You don't hit me like a gang banger or a terrorist . . . Do ya got another $300?" as he looked around to make sure no one could hear us.

"Yeah! I think so!" I started counting again. I need a box of shells for each of those. I threw down a fifty-dollar bill. He slapped two boxes of 44's, a case of 12GA shells, and a box of deer slugs.

"That do it?" He asked.

"Almost! . . . . Hey!" I turned to a table across from him . . . . "What do you want for those gulf clubs?"

"It would be a steal at $100 . . . ." and he started his sales pitch.

"Fifty gonna do it?" as I waved the bill in his face.

He grabbed it, and I drug the clubs over to the gun dealer. I dumped the golf balls into the trash and dropped the 44 Magnum into the ball pocket. I pulled a sock off a 9 iron, put it over the end of the shotgun, and stuffed it into the bag. I dropped the remaining shells into the bag, rolled the whole thing out to the Cherokee, and put them in the back.

I drove back to the airport and found the rental car that Michigan would be taking in the morning. I hid the 44 behind the spare tire in the trunk. I bought a *pay as you go* phone at the airport booth and had it activated on the spot. I called Michigan on the way to the hotel on I-95.

RRrrrring . . . RRRRrring . . . . "You dialed the number, you know who I am. Leave a message and if I like it I may call you back!" *BEEP!*

"*It's me* .... *You're on Delta flight 4537 leaving Detroit later this evening at 9:17 PM. I realize I am cutting you close, but the car and the hotel are reserved and paid in advance by Saborio Fashions. You are an out of town buyer. The car is a black Lincoln Continental Lisc # AVI-357. They should just hand you the keys. I booked you for four days at the La Quinta at I-95 and Rt.713 starting today, suite #23. Your new toy is in our normal location wrapped in a generous expense account. I will call you at the hotel tomorrow at noon. Thanks again!*" Click!

I picked the speed up to 75MPH and threw the phone up over my roof. I watched it smash to pieces as the car behind me ran over it. I drove back to my house and pulled into the garage.

"Hi Julie! Everything okay?" I ask.

She wiped her eyes from sleeping on the couch.

"Oh yes! Daniel is no trouble at all."

"I really appreciate you helping me out!" I handed her $50.00

She smiled and stood to go out the door.

"Julie ... Has anybody come around or called since I was gone?"

"No! Everything has been quiet! Your mail is on the table! Bye!" and she went out the door.

I went down the hall and looked at Daniel sound asleep. There was still an unmarked car on the street under my neighbor's big tree. I went out in the driveway, raised the hatch of the Cherokee, and rolled the golf clubs into the house. I set them against a big chair, near the front door, where I could grab the shotgun in a hurry if necessary. I took my laptop into the living room, pulled up an old email address that I do not use any more, and composed a letter to Loren.

Loren,

I am planning a visit to stay with you and momma.
Daniel and I will arrive in the next few days. I will call
you when we arrive. DO NOT try to contact me or Lisa!
I will explain everything later.
    We are anxious to see you!

Love,
Jonah

I called the detective whose card I still carried in my money clip.

"Hello . . . Detective O'Malley! This is Jonah Bradford. I plan on taking my son on a short vacation to visit his family in Costa Rica. Am I still being investigated or is it okay to leave the country for a few days?"

"No sir, your alibis all checked out. Will I be able to reach you at this same cell phone number?" The detective asks firmly.

"Yes! I keep it close most of the time."

"Okay . . . . Go ahead . . . and I appreciate you checking in with us! Good evening!"

"Bye!" *click!*

I went back on line and ran a search on *remote camera public access feeds.* I was amazed at how many cameras there were all up and down the interstate and at various locations of the cities. I kept detailing my search until I found a live feed from the immigration office on the pier at the marina. The Uncle Tom was clearly visible. Maybe they were already watching him? I locked in this camera on my internet favorites, turned off the laptop, and went to bed.

Daniel, by some miracle, slept the entire evening.

*   *   *

I called Julie at 8:00 and ask her to babysit again.

"Julie ... Would you mind picking up some breakfast from McDonalds on the way for us both?" I begged.

She showed up about the time I was shaved, dressed and ready for another day. I spent the morning in my boat working on some new ideas for my book and going over the details of the next few days. At noon I borrowed Julie's phone again and called La Quinta, suite #23. Michigan answered the phone.

"Yeah!" He said.

"Everything go okay?" I asked

"Yeah! I have already picked up all the ingredients for the cake. It should be ready to be delivered to the wedding by tomorrow morning. Will that be adequate?"

"Yes! Have you checked the route for the delivery and researched which room the reception will be in?"

"Yes! My bakery only provides the finest service!" Said Michigan.

"The wedding will be broadcast on this internet site."

I spelled the remote camera address, knowing that he was recording the call.

"Interesting! Can you make a personal appearance?"

"At your bakery?" I asked.

"Yes."

"Would 2:30 be too soon?"

"That will be fine! Pick up some cold Michelob on the way .... BOTTLES!" He chuckled.

"2:30!" *click.*

I told Julie that I had to do some running and that I may be late. She said if it goes too late, she'll sleep in the bedroom next to Daniel's.

"I really do appreciate this Julie!" and I ducked into the garage.

I monitored traffic carefully as I drove to La Quinta. I stopped and got gas. I stopped again later and bought the beer, just to double check for a tail. I pulled into the La Quinta and parked in the back. I walked around the end of the building and up the steps to suite #23. The door opened as I raised my hand to knock.

"How's it hang'n dude?" as he pulled a Michelob from the bag and popped the top.

"It's seen better days." I pulled a cold one out too.

"Hey . . . . Sorry about your ole lady. That sucks! But retribution has arrived."

He pointed to the miles of wires all over the counter tops in the kitchen.

"Tell me about this." I said.

"Okay . . . This is the most important part" as he pointed to a dozen little zip-lock packages of white powder.

"These . . . are my own creation." He said proudly.

"When one of *these*, ignites one of these little bags with the pull off sticky backs . . . then the white shit completely ignites in less than a second."

"And you have 12 bags of that stuff, which will all ignite simultaneously?" I asked.

"Correctamundo!" He seemed very pleased.

"El Problamo . . . . There is going to be a lot of innocent people around this freighter and I don't really want a large explosion!" I said with a worried look on my face.

"Oh ! I left out the best part!!!! Each of these little bags has an ignition spread of only 10'. The beauty is that each one burns at 6000 deg. AND . . . arrives at that temperature in less than a second. I stick six of these on each side of his mattress, under his sheet, and ignite it after he goes to sleep. Poof!" and he smiles at me.

Oh!!! He'll burn to ashes right in his mattress, and not even have time to wake up!" I injected.

"Exactly!" as he stroked the end of his grey goatee.

So how do we ignite it?" I asked.

"Oh!!! Oh!!! That's cool too!!!! The fuck'n cell phone!"

He showed me a pay as you go phone with the back open. The speaker wires had been disconnected and re-connected to a relay taped to the phone. The relay activated the string of igniters.

I slowly studied his system of wires following the current with my hands.

"So, you call this number ... from another disposable phone ... this phone rings .... and *flash?*" I confirmed.

"Right .... accept *YOU* call the number, and it goes *flash!*"

We both stood staring at each other as we continued to think it through.

"You still with me Captain?" Asked Michigan.

"Yes. So when can you install this?" I asked.

"I intend to have it armed before he goes to bed tomorrow evening."

He looked at me dead serious.

"*I like it!* Call my phone and let it ring two times and hang up before I answer. Make the call when it is all ready and you are about to get on the plane."

I handed him an envelope of money.

"It was a pleasure doing business with you Sir."

He shook my hand and I grabbed a Michelob for the road.

* * *

I booked a first class seat for a small child and myself to Costa Rica, for tomorrow morning.

I called Julie and told her I was on the way back and would she pack enough baby supplies for a one week vacation for Daniel and me?

I gave her another $50, thanked her again and told her to watch the house.

"We will settle up when I get back." I said.

In the morning Daniel and I were airborne to Costa Rica. I carried my disposable phone and my regular phone, in my laptop case. It was on my left shoulder. The baby stuff was on the other shoulder with Daniel in my arms. We hit the tarmac in Limon by 3PM and I called Loren on my regular phone to pick us up.

She was confused, and wanted to know where Lisa was. I convinced her to wait until we get to the house and put Daniel to bed.

Daniel went right to sleep, and we all sat at the kitchen table as I told the story. The crying was intense. I told them that I needed them to be strong. Loren was immediately in, because this man that I wanted to obliterate was the same man that kidnapped and beat her years ago.

Momma was a bit reserved, but compromised her morals when she realized that Lisa had been kidnapped, and raped when she was young and then years later, murdered by the same man. I flipped open my laptop and signed in to Loren's router. We clicked onto the live camera and the Uncle Tom appeared in *Real Time* on my screen. I laid the disposable phone on the table and explained that *this* will ignite *that*, as I pointed to the freighter.

"We just want him! So we have to wait until he goes to bed." I explained.

"I have a man working for me as we speak. When the phone rings, and stops, we are ready to proceed. So . . . for now we just wait."

I walked into the living room and watched TV, while Loren stared at the computer screen.

When the phone rang . . . *RRRRING* . . . . *RRRRING* . . . and then stopped, I knew Michigan was on the plane and everything was ready.

The screen showed it getting dark in Florida, and I couldn't call the other phone until Captain Raymond goes to bed. We attentively watched the monitor. We saw people leaving the ship and the Captain turning off the lights. He stayed in his room until late, watching TV. Finally he got up and visited the bathroom, turned off the lights, and went to bed.

We all looked at each other and I started dialing the number on my key pad. I hesitated at the last number and waited . . . . I looked into Loren and momma's eyes.

"What's the last number?" Asked Loren.

"Seven"

She reached across the table and pushed 7.

Nothing happened for a few minutes. I started to get worried, and then . . . . his cabin glowed like the sun from inside. The camera went to static, as it was unable to handle the intense light. We stared at the computer screen as it finally came back on, to show the center of the metal roof had melted into a hole above Raymond's Cabin. As the intense light faded to flickering flames, the entire ship exploded. The flames danced on the water as the surrounding boats moved away to a safe distance.

We read about the explosion on the Florida Channel 9 News, on the internet. The story said that;

> *The fire was caused by the floating meth lab that he ran below deck. They also found evidence of drug trafficking and Human Trade, from the safe that remained in the hull below water level. The vessel had melted to water level and the investigators related the intense heat to the drug production ingredients. The Captain was incinerated beyond recognition.*

We all went to bed, although none of us slept. We got up in the morning and booked a return flight for all five of us. We had to prepare for Lisa's funeral.

Chapter 13

I did a mass mailing to all of our suppliers and franchise owners. I explained the general details of Lisa's murder. I assured them that their supply of original Saborio Product would continue, and I re-introduced Georgia Burns that had been working with Lisa for the past year.

I did a private letter to Gloria in St Croix, Jim Monelle, the textile company in Costa Rica, and Bello Fashions, which got this all, started.

The funeral would be next Saturday and I let the funeral director make all the arrangements. While he dealt with that, I put the boat back in the water and brought it back up to my dock.

*   *   *

I could not believe the attendance. Everyone that I emailed showed up with everyone they had forwarded the email to. I made an emergency call to the catering service at my house, and instructed them to add more food!

I was very surprised when Gloria from St Croix showed up and wanted to meet Daniel. She knew about him at the same time I did. I invited her to stick around after the funeral and visit a few days. She accepted, and that occupied my last bedroom.

I was useless at the funeral. All of the hatred that I used for fuel for the last few weeks, had drained off now and the suppressed emotion kept trying to surface. The guests probably thought I had a bladder infection with as many trips as I made to the restroom to dry my eyes and regroup.

I stood at her casket and looked at her in her favorite creation. *The Black Teaser Dress.* I even let the director use her black diamond necklace and ear rings until after the funeral. I pulled a small bottle from my jacket pocket marked AMARETTO, and pushed it into her hand.

"You're welcome!" I said aloud, and then walked away.

There were 96 cars in the funeral procession, and that did not even include the people that pulled off the side of the road and stood beside their cars as we passed. The story had been on the news and in the papers.

All of the family finally broke down at the cemetery and this provoked other friends to lose it too. With no bathroom to run to, I buried my face in my handkerchief as Loran, and our boys climbed into the limo.

On the way to my house, we cheered each other up by talking about our guests and some of the clothes they were wearing.

You could tell she was in the fashion business, as a large percentage of the people appeared to be looking for a Fashion Runway. They evidently thought they could strut their favorite getup across the sand and grass in their stilettos.

The women, *Loren and momma,* touched up their make-up as we parked in front of the house.

To add to the wall-to-wall people, most of my neighbors showed up. I doubt the catering service will ever work for me again. They could not leave until 3AM and then had to search for people to move their cars that were blocking them in. I had people sleeping in my floor and in all of the bedrooms. Momma and Gloria had their doors locked. I even had people I did not know sleeping in the mother-in-laws apartment above the garage. It had not even been cleaned.

There were cars on the road, in my driveway, and even in on my grass.

I woke up in the master cabin of my boat. I looked down at the head on my shoulder and gently kissed Loren on the forehead. We were both still completely dressed and still exhausted. Loren sat up in a big hurry and said:

"Have you checked on the boys?" Loren quickly got off of the bed.

"No!" as I tried to remember where we left them?

She came back and crawled back on the bed.

"They're still asleep."

Then I remembered that they were in the V-berth.

Loren laid her head back on my chest, and we slept a little while longer.

* * *

The boys woke up at 9am. Daniel needed attention as David made fun of him and ran for the house. As we migrated back indoors there were only a few people left and momma and Georgia were serving breakfast to everyone.

"You better get it while you can . . . this is the last of your groceries!"

Momma scooted a cup of coffee in front of me.

With everyone served and gone, *or going*, we survivors emptied the last pot of coffee and went out to the pool with our reward. It was a cool morning. That means it was only 72 deg. so far, and I looked around at the faces that I knew mattered.

Most of us went back to bed and did not show our faces until noon. Momma could not stand the condition of the house and had it all spotless by the time we got up.

I watched the news, *still* showing footage of the freighter fire, and watched David trying to teach Daniel how to fart M&M's.

"Definitely my boys!" I thought.

After a few more days, Loren and I took Gloria to the airport. She hugged me and moved to Loren. While she hugged Loren, her eyes got watery. You are so much like Lisa, as she glanced at me and smiled.

She waved goodbye, walked into the customs door, and we headed for home.

As we drove around the circle of Orlando International, and exited onto Rt. 528, I looked over at Loren.

"I don't know if you noticed, but I didn't book any return flight for you."

"Actually, I did notice!" She said, "I figured you had a plan."

"If I could get your green cards, would all of you consider staying in the United States?"

"And do what?" She asked.

"You know I am out of my league with Daniel. I definitely need help. This way the boys could grow up together, and I could be a *father* to David, instead of Uncle Jonah!"

"So would we all live at your house?" She asked.

"Sure! We can let momma have the mother-in-law apartment, and she can still baby sit and hang out with us any time she wants."

"You said us? Define that for me?" as she got serious.

Right now I am still not over Lisa. I cannot get the *bathtub* picture from my mind. I am sure it will get better eventually, and I am smart enough to know that you are the only woman I will ever want. I was in love with you from the beginning. Momma even knew! BUT!!!! Right now I am not quite ready to start anything else. Do you understand?"

"Completely! I would like to stay, and I will talk to momma." Loren answered.

Once again momma already knew this would happen and informed us that she had listed the house in Costa Rica with a Realtor before she left.

Momma, Loren and David flew back to Cost Rica while I worked on the apartment, and thought through all the pros and cons of my decision. Two weeks went by and the longer they were gone the more I realized I could have it no other way. I was sleeping, and working, in the boat while Daniel slept in the V-berth. Somehow the boat felt tighter than the big empty house.

I kept the TV going in the background and Daniel and I talked *as much as we could* ... about how our lives were about to undergo another change. He did not seem to care one way or the other but I think explaining it all to him worked like therapy for me. To him, Loren *is* Lisa. I caught myself looking for her, excited, each time Daniel strung together a few more words into a sentence.

* * *

I hired a maid service to spend the day at the house before Daniel and I went to the airport to pick up the family. Everything was clean, and working, and I had cable and internet installed into momma's apartment. We took the Cherokee, drove it through a car wash, and headed for the airport. As I looked out across the marshland to the side of I-95, I realized that I had not been thinking of Lisa. I had been thinking about Loren. I smiled and realized that my life was experiencing gradual corrections, and it felt ... *right.*

I pulled into Banyan Air, and parked against the chain link fence. Loren chose a small commuter jet from Orlando to save me such a long drive. Daniel stood with his fingers squeezing the wires in the fence as Loren walked toward us smiling. We all walked along the fence as they went inside the building. Daniel and I continued to the front entrance to wait. Momma came out first and hugged me as she rocked me back and forth like a child.

"You're a good man Jonah." She said.

I patted her on the back as Loren butted in and squeezed me even harder. She rubbed her bare knee between my legs as I felt ... *firmness occurring.*

"Okay! Let's get this troop loaded and head for the house." I said trying to take my mind off Loren's beautiful legs.

She smiled and took my hand. David walked proudly beside me and momma walked slowly with Daniel.

On the way back, everyone in the back seat went to sleep. Loren kept smiling at me as I told her all the things Daniel and I did while we were alone. I several times reached over and squeezed her hand and I know she realized that I had missed her. The first night back was equally as exciting. Everyone was tired and stressed. By 8:30 everyone was asleep, except me. I sat in the Saborio and typed into the laptop until 3AM. I had a lot of new input for my manuscript.

*   *   *

Loren and momma's belongings had been shipped in a small sea container and would arrive in a few weeks. I emptied the third bay of the garage so that they could unload it as slowly as they wanted, when it arrived.

Although the apartment was immaculate, it had no personality. The women took this opportunity to go shopping.

Loren and momma shopped for days decorating the new apartment and setting up a private bedroom for David in the main house. If he had his way, he would live on the boat. They decorated his room to look as much like a boat as possible. David and I both just shook our heads and headed for the channel. It just was not the same without the rocking of the waves.

Daniel was starting to follow around his new brother, and finally the green cards were approved with me as the joint group sponsor. Loren still slept in her room and I in mine. Her constant presence made the adjustment *without Lisa* go much faster. I still occasionally had trouble with the loss of Lisa.

They not only looked identical, but also had a lot of the same little habits. Nothing important ... just little things like letting her flip-flops drag as she walked across the pool deck. Things that used to bother me, were missed now.

Loren was not really interested in the business. Georgia was doing a fine job, and all the buyers loved her, so we just left it alone.

I discovered that Loren is a painter. As a gift she painted me a beautiful oil painting of the Saborio and I hung it above my headboard in the master bedroom. She was teaching David and he was quite good too. He was always bringing me things he drew and I was always impressed.

Sometimes I had to work on the boat and I started taking David with me to hand me tools and learn mechanical things. He learned fast and several times, we went home greasy and sweaty as Loren smiled at us both and cleaned him up. I bought him his first bike and taught him how to ride it. Loran took him to school every day. We traded in the Cherokee for a Land Rover LR2 and Loren said that it was *hers*. Life was getting back to . . . . *normal for us* . . . . and one day when I went home, momma was sitting at my dining room table waiting for me.

"Come here Jonah! You know that Momma Saborio knows all . . . . right?"

I smiled at her . . . "Right!" as I leaned back in my chair.

"You are not getting any younger! It has been almost a year since Lisa died. You have grieved long enough! You are in love with my Loren . . . . Right?"

"Yes." as I thought deeply.

"So . . . you are wasting your lives being apart. What is the problem?"

"I am afraid that I am looking at Loren and still seeing Lisa. I don't want to ruin Loren's life, living in the shadow of her sister." I stared at the table.

"There are so many things about Loren you still have not discovered. You had no idea that she was a painter, did you?"

"NO! I didn't."

"Well . . . . There is still a lifetime of surprises for you to discover, and she is patiently waiting for you to find them. She loves you Jonah!"

I continued staring at the table like a punished child.

"*I have an idea,*" Momma said, as I looked up at her, "I will take care of the boys and the house. Take Loren, get in your boat, and just GO! Do not make any plans. Just pack your clothes and supplies and toss a coin for which way to set your sails. See what happens?" She got up from the table and left me to think about what she said.

After David got home from school, I got him to help me wax and clean the boat. It hadn't been used in a long time. We worked on it for a week and I gave David some money for helping me. He was very good with the detail areas that drive me crazy.

A few days later, everyone was asleep and the house was dark. I lay in my bed thinking again of momma's words. I stood and put on my robe and walked across the hall to Loren's room. I opened the door and could hear her breathing as I followed the sound in the dark. I felt her shoulder and lay down beside her. She woke up feeling, my breath on her neck. She reached out with her hand and touched my face.
"Jonah, What are you doing in here?" Came a sleepy voice.
"I couldn't sleep. I want to go sailing. Just the two of us!"
"Where?"
"I don't know? We'll flip a coin and see where we end up!"
She pushed her face toward me and kissed me on the lips.
"And when are we going to leave?" She asked.
"When you wake up in the morning"
I kissed her again and went back to my bedroom.

Chapter 14

Loren was up early packing her clothes and packing everything she thought she might need on the boat. She wanted to drive in to her favorite art store and pick up a few tubes of oils that she was running low on. I asked her to stop by Sam's and pick us up a big bag of Duncan Donut Coffee.

"Jonah!!! When will we be back?" Asked Loren.

"No idea!" as I smiled at her.

She hesitated for a second and then smiled before jumping into her car and backing onto the pavers.

"So . . . Jonah! *You are going on a vacation?*" Momma smiled from ear to ear.

"Yes! I wish I could say it was all my idea!"

"Well if Loran asked you . . . it was!" She hugged me and poured a cup of coffee.

"Are you going to be okay with the boys?" I asked.

"Oh yes . . . Don't worry about us! You just go pull this family together!" as she took another sip. "Everything is going to work out like one of your *romance stories!*" She said.

"You think so?"

"*Momma Saborio knows so!*" She smiled and went down the hall to wake up the boys.

As I watched her feed and dress them I knew they were in expert care.

"If you need a trip to the grocery or help for anything . . . here's a phone number for our babysitter. She has a car, and is very reliable. I always overpay her so keep it up."

Loran returned and pulled into the garage. We finished stocking the boat then hugged the boys, and told them to mind Momma Saborio. We promised to email them pictures and David had a computer in his room now. I had set up restricted access on it so he did not end up sex crazy like his Daddy.

They all stood around the pool as we cast off and motored down the channel. We waved, motored into the big channel, and were now out of sight. We were sad to leave the boys but we both felt a new life starting and were eager to get to it.

I was a bit nervous about a lot of things. I had not been on the ocean in almost a year and I had not been with a woman in that time either. As we carefully motored through St. Lucie Inlet, the wind picked up and the watercolor darkened. I unfurled the jib and then the main. The wind filled the sails of the Saborio as she heeled over and jumped through the swells.

"Which way?" I asked as the water got deeper.

"Heads . . . East . . . tails . . . South . . . she flipped a quarter. She kept her palm on it and I moved to see the results."

"EAST!" She said.

"I was already headed east so I just locked in the autopilot and adjusted the sails. I sat down in the Captains seat. She leaned against me and smiled at the ocean ahead of us. We continued into the evening and with a slight variation of our course, we were on target for Grand Bahamas Island. We stayed up together until she got sleepy. She brought a pillow and blanket into the cockpit, and slept on deck while I was on watch. I caught myself dozing off about 1AM and woke her up for her shift. I crawled into her warm blanket and was out in five minutes.

She woke me up at 4:30 and I finished the course into the sunrise. I kicked on the autopilot, went below, and made coffee and bagels with peanut butter. I woke her up, and she sat with the blanket wrapped around her. She let me get a few hours sleep before she wanted me to bring it in to the commercial zone.

*   *   *

We anchored out and took the dingy into town to shop. We had fun looking at things together and she encouraged me to pick things out that I would like to see her wear. It was sort of like foreplay for my imagination. Before we went back to the boat, she picked up some steaks and took them back to the boat for tonight.

We had anchored around the point from the shopping area. It was only fifteen feet deep with a small private beach. The beach was only accessible from the water due to the big jagged rocks that shot out of the sand like a row of decaying monoliths. We swam around the boat and over to the beach to explore and lie in the sun. We lay in the sand with the warm water massaging our bodies. As the sun set behind our stones, it created a shadow on the water. The sun was still illuminating the boat and Loren said she would like to paint this scene if we have time. We swam back to the boat and she put the steaks on the charcoal that had been glowing now for about an hour.

We ate on deck and drank wine with our diner. The mosquitoes finally arrived as we finished, and we went below and put the screens in the portholes. Loren got ate up, and I started rubbing olive oil on her bites as she lay on her tummy on the bed. I found bites all over her body. Some even got under her clothes which had to be removed to treat. I was really starting to enjoy this part of our trip.

She found several similar bites on me and even one that was swollen and required specialized treatment.

"OOooohhhhhhh!"

"Both of us had been sexually deprived for almost a year now. Over the next two days we were only seen on deck occasionally to make sure the anchor did not drag.

Rain came in on the third day and extended our below deck time another 24 hours. We were both so relaxed now that if it was not for the kids, we would probably never go home.

The next day the sun was back where it belonged and Loren took the dingy and paddled over to the beach to do her painting. She liked to work alone, so I remained on the boat and connected to the internet. I took a digital picture of *Mommy Painting*.... and sent it to David and told him to show it to Daniel and Grandma.

Beneath the photo I typed a line, *"Right on Schedule!"* and I told David exactly where we were and to mark it on the ocean chart that I gave him.

We left Grand Bahamas Island and headed south, as the quarter landed on *tails*. We ended up on a group of little islands called the Berry Islands. I had never been here before but we found an interesting spot on Cat Island and stayed there several days snorkeling and exploring the beaches and jagged rocks.

I took another photo of Loren walking on the beach in a bikini and a Java wrap. I saved it for the next email.

We had some tourist boats arrive and cramp our scantily dressed style, so we bid them farewell, flipped the coin again, and ended up at Great Harbor. We restocked a few supplies and flipped the coin.

After a very long day sailing, we found ourselves at Nassau. The traffic was heavy and I was on watch for freighters and cruise ships. We called ahead for dock space and went into town like civilized folks. I had dress shirts and slacks in the closet, but Loren felt she needed a new dress.

She knew from past experience that I was partial to *black*, and Loren went all out. She bought a short black dress with a V-neck that almost touched her naval. She wore black heels and accentuated her dark eyes with extra eye shadow and mascara. She hung a black beaded necklace into the cleavage, and framed it all in with her almost black, long, hair. I had to get a photo for myself. David would not see this one!

I was ready to stay on the boat and play, but she was insistent that we go out *for a change*. We started at a local casino and I had some drinks while Loran pulled the slot machines.

"AAAAHHHH!!!!" as the coins dropped into the floor. She dropped to the floor chasing all the coins. Her dress went up, exposing her beautiful legs. She had no idea how horney she was making me. She was ready to move on, as her black purse bulged with the coins. She cashed them in for paper money that fit her purse better. We walked down the street and she heard a band that she recognized from Costa Rica. They played Salsa and she pulled me into the club to watch the live band. Everyone was dancing and the body movements were very erotic. Loran wanted to dance.

"Come on . . . dance with me!" She begged.

"I don't know how!"

"You don't have to know how . . . you just move your body to the feelings!" as she drug me onto the floor.

She danced around me like a personal lap dance. This dancing was about the next thing down from foreplay. I watched a few of the other men and started moving like they did. Loran moved around me, grabbed me when she needed to, and made it look like I knew what I was doing.

She was sliding up and down my body, and sliding my knee between her legs. She kept holding her hemline down. It kept creeping up as she danced. She moved away from me and put on a very sexy show directed to me alone.

She was soooo sexy!

I moved toward her as I became her *stripper pole* and she almost made me forget that we were not alone. She was ready to go now and I was glad. She was attracting a few male admirers from the tables.

We continued down the street letting the ocean breeze cool our bodies back down. Hers, from all the dancing, and mine, from watching her dance. We went into a VERY nice restaurant, and were seated by a waiter in a tux. It was a dark restaurant and had quiet music in the background from a live piano player. He sat us at a C-shaped cove with a round table. The light was supplied by a single candle on the table, with a burgundy tablecloth that went to the floor. We sipped on our wine and studied the menu as the waiter watched from a distance. I laid the menu down and he appeared like a Jeanie, ready to take our order. Loran ordered shrimp, while I ordered Steak Dianne.

They cooked my meal at the table with brandy and a torch. It shot flames to the ceiling. Loran jumped and scooted against me. I placed my hand on her leg sliding her dress up as far as I could without being obvious. She wasn't wearing panties. As we waited for the food I played with the smooth area between her legs. She leaned her head on her hand as if we were talking.

About the time that she was starting to make little noises, the waiter delivered the remaining food. We regrouped and took our time, eating our dinners like *grown-ups*.

"Can I interest you in desert?" as he took our plates.

"Do you have fried brandy plantains?"

"I can have the chef prepare that if you're not in a big hurry?"

I looked at Loren and she motioned to go ahead . . .

"But just make one! . . . we will share it!" She said.

"Coffee?" He asked.

"Please . . . two . . . one with amaretto." I looked at Loren.

"NO! I like *hazelnut!*" She said, and the waiter headed for the kitchen.

Our coffee was delivered and Loran was looking around at all the empty tables. The business was really slowing down. We had both been drinking a better quality wine than usual and the effects were starting to show. Loren smiled at me and slid under the tablecloth. I felt her hand on my zipper. I slid down in my seat and tried to look casual. She was making me crazy.

"Here is you plantains Sir, with two forks" as he placed it in front of me.

"Has your companion left?"

He looked toward the front door.

"In the ladies room" I said.

He nodded his head and laid the check down.

I reached below the tablecloth and reluctantly pulled Loran back into her seat.

"Oh desert has arrived?" as she grabbed a fork.

We devoured the desert and left the waiter a generous tip for leaving us alone. We walked back to the dingy, and to show how classy we were, Loren stood up in the bow of the dingy holding the bow line for stability while she giggled. I was more concerned about the heels and our inflatable's missing puncture kit. We found our boat and I switched on the anchor light.

We went to the master cabin as Loren climbed up on the bed and held her foot out to me. I removed her heel and she held up the other foot giggling. She rolled over and I unzipped the long zipper down her back. She pulled it up over her hips and sat up as I removed it over her outstretched arms. I started removing my clothes. She rolled over on her tummy. I admired her tight waist and rounded buns.

I stepped out of my pants, and started licking, from her ankles to her hips. I spent a few minutes there before proceeding up her body. I penetrated her gently lying on her back as I nibbled on her neck. She made cooing sounds while I moved my hips from side to side. She raised her buns a bit and I achieved deeper penetration. She moaned louder. I rolled her over and her knees went against her breasts.

"Jonaaah!!! Jonaaaah!!" She whispered.

"Yes?"

"I want another baby." She said from nowhere.

I pulled out and rolled over onto my back as she put her head on my shoulder.

"Aren't we getting a little ahead of things?" I said as my erection deflated.

"Maybe . . . . but I do! Sooner or later you are going to figure out that you have always loved me, and I have always loved you. We have each taken the long way around getting here . . . . but here we are! We already have a son together, and I am perfectly willing to raise Lisa's son as my own. I think momma likes you better than me now, so what is keeping us from making all of this . . . real?" She asks with a serious look.

There was a long silence in the cabin as both of us faced each other on our sides with our elbows in the mattress, and our heads propped up on our hands. I stared into Loren's big brown eyes for a long time, *as she did not even blink.* I squinted my eyes at her and slowly flashed her a full smile.

"I can't think of a damn thing!"

We both broke out laughing and rolled around on the bed hugging each other.

The mood returned to both of us, and the day was finished with both of us exhausted again.

Now my life had a new purpose that I could really get into. *I need to make another baby!*

We spent the next week hopping from one beautiful bay to the next around three sides of Andros Island. I took a lot of pictures of Loren being investigated by the birds and sitting behind thousands of sea creatures. I was out of range to e-mail the photos to Florida, but we should have access when we get near Key West. Days later we cleared customs in Key West and left the Saborio tied to one of the *pay per day* mooring buoys that now seem to be appearing everyplace.

We went ashore, acted like tourists, and even rented a room in a hotel with an in room Jacuzzi. It was a very busy night after an alcohol instigated public foreplay incident. Don't ask!

Loren was inseminated repeatedly this evening. We broke in the bed, the balcony, the Jacuzzi, the roof, and the emergency stairway. I took a picture of the hotel as we left to show my next son where he was conceived. I was confident that Loren *had* to be with child now.

We slept until noon the next day and laughed about all the crazy things we did last night. We returned to the boat and got off of the mooring buoy before they charged us for another day.

We sailed up the Keys stopping at a giant marina in Miami. We only stayed overnight and made it as far as Boca Raton the next day. We anchored near a bridge and continued the next morning. We had an excellent wind and a bit of current that helped speed us in the right direction. We almost made it home but decided to not push it and try to do the inlet during the day. We anchored out again, near Hobe Sound, and spent our last night together on the boat.

There were a lot of hugging and cozy romantic moments. It was an easy cruise to Stewart and we tied on to our dock before sunset. David had spotted us coming up the channel and had a complete reception committee waiting for us. We had been gone almost two months now and you could tell we had been missed.

The boys dragged Loren into the house and wanted to show her all of the pictures that I had e-mailed back to them.

"Tell me about this picture! Where were you in this picture? What is that animal?" They inquired.

"I'll tell you all about it later . . . let me get in the house first."

They hung on her as if they were afraid she may leave again.

"Why are you on the roof of this building? . . . Why are you hanging over the edge?"

"Come on boys! Give her a break." I said.

She will have to break all the stories down to the PG versions.

Momma waited for me.

"So ... was the mission successful?" She asked.

She smiled at me as if she already knew the answer.

"Yeah! Loren and I are gonna make it all legal very soon!" I returned her smile.

"Well ... I guess you had better! She is already pregnant!"

I stopped walking. Momma Saborio continued walking toward the house and smiled back over her shoulder at me.

"How do you know these things?" I asked.

"I'm Momma Saborio ... remember?"

Chapter 15

I tried to make the point to Loren that we were already married.

"So ... we were just standing next to the wrong persons, but we said I do, at the same ceremony?"

It did not fly!

Getting serious, my next move required an attorney and a fat check. I wanted to naturalize my new family and at the same time have both of my boys be a Bradford, along with their new little brother. The lawyers had to acquire documentation on the complete settlement of papers and properties from Loran's divorce in Costa Rica, including documentation of her, and Lisa's, marriage in Costa Rica, and then document her as my wife in the US.

David would have to have a name change and would become American when his mother became my wife since I, his biological father, was already American or something like that?

They felt that a family DNA test would eliminate any doubt that the court my feel, but at the same time raise the question of my character.

They went to work on it and I took the entire family for an overnight sail to South Carolina. There was a bigger boat there that Jim Monelle called me about and it was owned by a yacht broker that would take a trade. The Saborio was still in mint condition, but it only had two big cabins with two heads. This prospect, a *Celestial*, had three cabins and crew bunks. It was also

54' and was fully restored and upgraded to current specs. We motored out into blue water and headed north.

As soon as the sails went up David was barfing his guts out. He could shoot it across the deck like a scene from the Exorcist. Lisa kept the water bucket full and rinsed the deck each time, waiting for him to get the dry heaves. Momma started feeling it too and I gave her prescription strength Dramamine and sat her on the stern next to me. After a half hour she was fine. She decided to continue taking it just to be safe. Daniel played below deck and kept falling against things.

Loran sat beside me remembering all of the good times we shared on this boat as we shot ESP thoughts back and forth at each other. It felt good having our *entire* family involved in our favorite activity this time.

The trip north was good for breaking in my inexperienced crew. The winds were steady and the Gulf Stream sped us along. Loren and I did our night watch routine in the cockpit as our guests slept in the V-berth. Having all three of them in the forward cabin was good for sleeping under sail. We did not have to worry about them falling out of bed in the V-berth.

I watched Loren more than I normally would, knowing that she is pregnant. She seemed to be totally unaffected by it so far, and if she carries the baby as Lisa did, it should be another easy childbirth. I really never planned on having kids and look at me now. Number three in the cooker! I still cannot believe it myself.

"Loren . . . See the ship lights over there?" as I pointed.

"Yes! That is weird!" She said.

"Will you go below and look them up in the Chapman's book, and see what we're dealing with."

She returned about five minutes later with a flashlight showing me what she found.

"Okay . . . . fisherman! Looks like they have a net out. See if you can raise them on the radio?"

"Here!" as she took the helm. "You go talk to them!" and she scooted me out of my seat.

I laughed and went below.

"Fishing Vessel, Fishing Vessel . . . . Saborio, Saborio, over!"

"Saborio . . . Gorden . . . Gorden . . . go to 72, over."

I switched to channel 72. David had come from the V-berth and was studying my every move.

"Gorden . . . this is sailing vessel Saborio. Do I understand you to be multiple fishing vessels, probably with a net in the water? Over!"

"That is correct Saborio. It would be advisable for you to alter course to N-NE until we pass, at which time you could resume your present course. Over!"

"Understood . . . Altering course to N-NE . . . over!"

"Thank you Saborio . . . we appreciate the consideration! Over and out!" . . . *click, click*

Click . . . click

"Loren! Bring us around tighter into the wind on a N-NE course. I will adjust the sails as you do it."

"Can I help?" Came a voice from behind me.

"Sure . . . you go steer the boat so Mommy can help me!" Loren looked at me concerned.

"Just show him compass bearings!" I said, "He can handle it!"

She started pointing to the numbers on the compass and was showing him how the numbers moved backwards to the wheel.

She then moved to the companionway and released the halyard as I reefed the main.

"Okay . . . winch it back in!" I said climbing into the cockpit.

Tick. tick. tick . . tick . . tick . . . . tick . . . . tick . . . . tick . . "Perfect!"

I walked back to the captain's seat, looked at the numbers on the compass, and took a glance at the chart plotter. I looked at David and smiled as I gave him thumbs up. I sat down, put my arm around Loren, and she snuggled against me.

"Good job Captain!" I grabbed the binoculars and checked the fishing fleet. It was 2AM and I winked at Loren and then looked at David. Isn't it time for a watch change?" I asked loudly.

"Yes! It's your shift!" She said. "David . . . It's time for you to get some sleep. Thanks for the help."

With his eyes blinking open and shut, he proudly made his way down the steps and back into the V-berth. He did not move until he heard us eating breakfast on our approach to Charleston.

We called the yacht broker that Jim gave us, on the cell phone, and he directed us to a dock outside of his office. My keel was about three foot off the bottom and the tide was still going out. I left the depth sounder on and monitored the decreasing number.

We cleaned up the boys, and momma volunteered to take them shopping at the marina shops.

Loren and I went ashore and sat down at the broker's desk. He knew we were coming and had everything printed up for us and a map showing where each boat was located.

"Monelle said he thought you might be interested in this one." as he laid the specs to the Celestial in front of us.

"Nice lines!" but the cabin layout isn't going to get it!" I said ... "A few things have changed since I bought my last boat from James! I have two small boys and a third one on the way." I smiled at Loren.

"Well Captain ... *congratulations* .... Are you working on getting your own crew?" He chuckled.

"Actually my oldest one helped sail on the way up here. He's only six!"

I caught myself bragging like the fathers I used to scoff at.

"Okay ... so you need some family space. That eliminates these two. Check this out!" as he slid me an Island Packet with a *private office*.

"I need to see that one! What else do you have on the property?"

"This one is over on the lot! It's a Passport! It's not cheap, but it's a world cruiser!"

"Okay ... give me the papers on that one too!"

After climbing in and out of hot boats all day we had not felt the love that I always feel when the match is right. All the things that I felt were wrong .... was already right on my Hylas.

In the end, we thanked the Broker and told him that we were just going to keep our own boat.

He was disappointed and confided in us that he had planned to take the Hylas for himself, and that he thinks that we made the right decision . . . unfortunately!"

The final deciding factor was that the Hylas was paid off and there were going to be more child expenses in the future. My overhead at the house had doubled since I brought everyone from Costa Rica, and momma was asking for a balcony on her apartment so she could sit outside and see the channel.

"I vaguely remember when life was so simple. Eat, drink, type, sail, and sex. Usually not in that order!"

Our Broker let us spend the evening on his dock and we went into town to the Dinosaur Museum. Momma and Loren were equally impressed and explained that they did not have things like this in Costa Rica. I followed our tour with an I-max movie and supper at Chucky Cheese.

I stopped and leaned against a basketball game as I looked at my overly excited family and thought about how lucky I was. In the same breath I panicked realizing that my original lifestyle of choice was gone forever. I kept having flashbacks of a comedian named Gallagher that drug an anchor with a diaper on it across the stage and informed the audience that his wife was pregnant.

With everyone exhausted, we called another taxi and headed back to the dock. We all squeezed into the back while momma rode in the front with the driver. We carried the boys down the dock to the boat. We made up beds for them in the main cabin. Momma had the V-berth to herself. Loren and I *shared* an unused marina shower before returning to the boat with all of the daily stress relieved.

We closed the galley way hatch quietly and stepped over the step that creaks. We slipped back into our cabin and shut the door softly in an effort to keep the crew asleep. We both stripped off our cloths and slipped under the sheets. I searched her tummy for my next son. After failing, I wiggled my finger into her belly button.

"Ding-Dong! . . . Hey! You in there?"

She pulled my hand onto her breast, and put her hand on top of mine.

"SShhhhhh. Go to sleep."

We were waked up in the morning by the boys climbing onto our bed, putting their faces against ours, and breathing loudly into our faces.

"Are you awake?" Asked David.

"We both faked a deep sleep until we grabbed them, pushed them down onto the sheets, and tickled them.

"AAAaahhh!" *Giggle* . . . *Giggle* . . . "AAAAaaaahhh!" *Giggle.* "Ha . . ha . ." *Giggle* . . . "Quit! . ha . . ha . . QUIT!!" Rang through the boat.

"Come on boys! Let them get up and get dressed. You help me make breakfast!" Said momma.

She pulled the cabin door shut and Loren and I pulled some sailing clothes from the closet. The smell of amaretto came through the door. Loren smiled at me and left the cabin.

*   *   *

David and Daniel played in the cockpit while momma and Loren cleaned the cabins and stowed everything for the trip. I ran the diesel charging the batteries, checked the fuel, and topped off the water tanks. With everyone on deck, and all five of us accounted for, we backed out of the dock and idled our way back out to blue water.

Daniel finally got his sea legs and spent more time on deck. We included David more and more in navigation and operation as we saw him understanding things. I think he will be my main sailor someday. Daniel wants to do everything David does but gets angry with us when we make him sit down and call him *shark bait*.

Shortly into our trip the clouds came in. The wind became very erratic and cold, and the Gulf Stream seems to have moved again. I went further offshore to try to find friendlier water. We had a few thunderstorms that made me nervous and I spent a lot of time on deck feeling more secure with my tether and vest on. Loren kept bringing me coffee and offering to help, but I just sent her below, to administer Dramamine, and keep our landlubbers calmed down and undamaged.

The sea cut me some slack at the next morning's sunrise. The swells had dropped to five feet and the wind became steady. I was chilled to the bone when momma brought me up a hot breakfast and sat with me drinking her *Amaretto with coffee.* Loren got the boys dressed and brought them up to the cockpit table. They looked like no one had slept and were both annoyingly grouchy.

* * *

With Port St. Lucia in the cross hairs, it was only another couple hours until we would be home.

It was an exhausting trip for me, but everyone else had a good time, and I had rekindled my love for my boat. After a few hours of sleep at home, I was back on my feet. The noise in the house had returned to operating mode. I grabbed my laptop and headed for the Saborio. I added some of this week's experiences in the finishing pages of the book that my publisher has been threatening me for. It needed a few more chapters to wrap things up, and I think it will soon be ready for the editor.

Loren came out to the dock in her bikini with a t-shirt over it. She kicked her flip-flops off and stepped aboard. She came below, scooted next to me, and was reading what I had typed.

She started laughing and distracted my thoughts. She smiled at me, *as I looked at her as I do* . . . when I am interrupted.

"Well! It was funny!" She said, as she smiled and ran her hand up under my shorts. She leaned toward me and kissed me on the lips. My expression remained unchanged.

"The kids are asleep, and I need some grown-up time." She finally broke my stare.

I smiled and turned off the computer, took her hand, and headed for the master cabin. I closed the door and locked it. We have to lock the doors now!

It was the tension breaker that we needed, and we both went to sleep afterwards.

*   *   *

I woke a little while later and was leaning on my elbow admiring how beautiful she is. She sleeps so peacefully and securely. I put my hand on her tummy searching for signs of my future son. I spread my hand wide as I expected him to be touching me through her flesh.

"What am I going to name you?" I said quietly.

I looked up and saw that Loren was awake and had been watching me with her eyes all watered up.

"I guess we are going to have to work on that?" She said, as she put her hand on top of mine.

I brought my laptop onto the bed, signed in to the router, and we started going through web sites of baby names.

We started looking up names and after an hour of searching, we decided Darius would be our third name from the bible.

"Loren . . . Why did you name our first son David?" I asked.

"David in the bible lusted for Bathsheba. He had multiple wives, slept with other men's wives, and even had them killed so that he could take Bathsheba. God loved David so much that he forgave him for all of that. It says that David is considered to be God's friend. I figured since my baby was your son, he needed all the help he could get!"

"HaaHaaaa!!!! . . . HaaHaaaa . . . !"

"Okay!!" . . . as I bit her leg.

"AAAaahhh!!!"

"Daddy!!!! Are you in the boat!"

Loren and I scrambled for our clothes?

159

"Yes! Stay back on the dock!" as I sat the computer on the galley table.

I was always worried one of the boys would fall between the boat and the sea wall and drown or get crushed as the boat moved with the waves. I appeared on deck, stepped off by David, and knelt down by him as Loren came on deck.

Grandma said to tell you two that lunch is ready, and that you have been in the boat long enough!" He ran back to the house.

I kissed Loren affectionately as we both smiled and walked to the house.

After lunch I walked out to the mailbox to get the mail. Along with the normal bills that never seemed to stop, I had a big yellow envelope from our attorneys. I walked back into the kitchen, opened the envelope, and pulled all the contents out. On top was a letter that explained all of the discovery work that they had done, and that everything that they questioned about the feasibility of marriage and name changes was now in order. All of the enclosed forms needed to be signed where all of the yellow arrows were. There were other sticky arrows that needed to be signed and notarized by the individuals whose name was typed under it. I grabbed a black ink pen and started signing my name as instructed. There was a copy of Lisa's death certificate that I had to sign to verify its authenticity, and another that I signed verifying that Daniel was the son of Lisa and me. David Jimenez would become David Bradford at the same time that Loren's name was recorded as Bradford, after our marriage. Momma Saborio would become a US citizen after a short period of time with a green card, using me as her sponsor. After a period of time and an easy test, she would become Maria D. Saborio, a legal US citizen.

We signed everything that we could, there at the house, and set up an appointment at the attorney's office for Thursday afternoon. I loaded the entire family into Loren's LR2 and we invaded the attorney's office right on schedule. They took us into the conference room and closed the door behind us, as three attorneys and two paralegals beheld our arrival. We signed more papers and watched notaries slapping their stamp on everything. With everything checked and double-checked the attorneys regrouped all their paperwork and handed it to the paralegals that left the room with it.

"Okay Mr. Bradford . . . . the only loose end we have right now is that you and Miss Jimenez are not married. Will you be resolving that problem . . . post haste?" as he smiled at us.

"*I will handle that one myself!*" Said Momma Saborio.

We reloaded the car and drove back to the house discussing our marriage plans.

"Loren and I both, having been married before, thought we would just go to a justice of the peace and quietly make it legal." I said.

Momma about climbed out of the car.

"No daughter of mine is going to be married at a justice of the peace like some knocked up teenager." Momma shouted!

All the adults in the car started laughing. Loren reminded her that she is carrying her second child. Momma broke out laughing too, but still begged Loren to get married in a church of God.

"All your kids have Bible names . . . so why mess it up now?"

We gave up and told momma to find us a church that would marry us in a hurry.

Momma went to work as soon as we got home and we could have got married Friday, if she had her way. Loren did not want to wear her first wedding gown and had in fact left it in Costa Rica. Momma somehow knew that Lisa's wedding gown was still in storage in an airtight hanging bag out in the garage. She got the dress out and made a few baby alterations by herself.

*   *   *

The wedding was unannounced other than the application for the marriage license. It was scheduled for the following Saturday afternoon in a small stone church on the back streets of Stewart. We planned no reception and had paid the church extra to supply their wedding photographer. James Monelle was my best man, and we flew Gloria in from St. Croix to stand with Loren. David was in charge of the beautiful wedding ring that I had created for Loren, and our buyer, Georgia Burns, was coming with her husband as witnesses. Short and sweet with all of the legal paperwork finalized.

Loren and I felt like we had been married for 15 years already. This wedding felt a bit strange to both of us.

Saturday afternoon James and I went to the church and arrived early enough to make sure that everybody was there and things were in order. The minister had thrown in an organ player for free just to set the proper mood, *in his opinion*. As I walked around visualizing what all was about to happen I kept noticing people coming in and sitting down. At first I did not recognize any of the people and then a big man with dark glasses, curly gray hair, and a short goatee, walked right up the isle and hugged me like a grizzly bear.

"Michigan!!! How did you hear about this?" I asked.

"I had a weird message on my answering machine from Momma Saborio. It said Jonah and Loren are getting married and for me to be here today or she was gonna find me and kick my ass! I gotta meet that little woman!!!" He walked past me and sat down in the front row.

The people kept coming. Our old babysitter Julie showed up with her parents and her little sister. Paul from the airport came in and sat toward the back. We had 20 or 30 people from our franchises that showed up with another 20 or 30 people that we did not even recognize. Just as the music started playing, Detective O'Malley showed up with his wife. He shook my hand, and told me how pleased he was that my life was going in the right direction again.

"Jonah!! Get your ass up here! *IT'S SHOWTIME!!*" Came a voice from the front row.

"Michigan . . . this is a church!! Control yourself!" as I stepped onto the platform.

The . . . *here comes the bride* . . . started playing and everyone stood and watched Loren enter the room right behind Gloria.

She looked radiant as she walked down the aisle and they had buried the evidence of *Darius* beneath several silk ribbons. She looked absolutely beautiful with her long black hair falling across her shoulders. I faced her from the platform, as our eye contact never broke until I took her hand and she stood beside me.

The preacher read from the Bible and I thought about how complete my life was now. As soon as we're legal and recorded then all of my past, present, and future becomes *one*, and forgiven.

I looked past the Bible that the preacher was holding and was staring at Loren's legs that showed between the split in the front of her gown. I visualized her white thigh high hose and that she was probably not wearing panties.

"Daddy . . . DADDY!!" as David pushed her ring against my forearm and snapped me back to reality.

"I do!" I said, as Loren smiled, blushed, and shook her head at me. She knew exactly what I was thinking!

"And Loren, do you take Jonah . . . . death do you part?"

"She flashed me a sexy smile and looked me in the eyes . . . . *paused for paybacks* . . . . I do!"

"Congratulations I now pronounce you Loren and Jonah Bradford . . . . you can kiss your bride!"

And I did without reservation.

To our surprise not only did we have a church half full of people, but momma had convinced the local catering service to come back to the house and do it again. This time they parked on the street and rolled the food into the house on carts. It was a wild party and went on just like the last one.

"Momma!" *I hugged her,* "Thanks for all of this . . . it is unreal! How did you make contact with all of these people?"

"*Hey !! I'm Momma Saborio!* Haven't you learned yet? Seriously . . . . I got David to hack into your laptop and copy all of your contacts from your address book. Between that and your daily schedule book, I had a very thorough list." as she winked at me.

"And . . . . I'm not finished. Your bags are already packed and the limo is going to pick you up in an hour. I booked you round trip tickets to a private home on a little tiny island in the Bahamas for a week. I do not want to hear a word from you until you two get back. You know I can take care of the boys, and all you have to do is take care of my daughter!" as she hugged me again.

"Hey are you the little pipsqueak that thinks she's going kick my ass?" Said Michigan.

"This is the little lady!" I told him, as he walked toward her preparing his bear hug.

"Jonah . . . . JONAH!!!!!!!!" Momma screamed.

"Sorry momma! I have to get ready for my honeymoon!" and I sprinted down the hallway.

"AAAaahhhhh!!!!!!!"

Chapter 16

Once again Momma Saborio knocked us on our butts! We had no idea where she was sending us but at least this time it seemed a little more premeditated than flipping a coin. The limo dropped us at a small airport in Palm City and we reclined into a small twin-engine prop plane that only had room for 10 or 15 passengers. We made a short stop on Grand Bahama Island and there were only six of us that remained on the plane. We were airborne for possibly 45 min. until the plane descended again onto another small runway on another Island. I heard the pilot say something about Bight Airport. There was a taxi waiting for us that had our names on a piece of cardboard. He picked up our luggage and had us follow him to his green van. We drove what seemed like a long way rambling through plush vegetation that finally opened up onto a small peninsula with a two bedroom cottage right on the beach. I tried to pay the driver.

"No no no!!! I'm already paid!!!" But he still accepted a $10 tip, and carried our luggage up onto the porch. He gave me a card to call him when I was ready to leave, and advised me that the trip back to the airport was also included as part of my rental.

Loren and I explored the interior of the house and debated on whether or not to turn on the air conditioning. Being Floridians we decided to leave it off and just enjoy the ocean breeze that had the curtains flapping out into the room. We shed our landlubber clothes in a hurry and changed into our suits. The beaches were white and clean and the water was as transparent as glass. We had packed our own snorkel gear and there was a very healthy reef within swimming distance. We explored the water for about an hour and lay in the shallow water as I rest on my side playing with Loren's baby bump. We rinsed the saltwater off in the outside shower, climbed into a nearby hammock, and slept until late afternoon.

We needed to stock a few groceries so we rummaged around the property until we discovered two bicycles and started pedaling from the direction that we initially arrived. We had failed to read in the description, that our cottage was located on the far end of a 7-acre estate. We enjoyed the ride on the packed sand road, but my butt was getting sore, and I was worried about what effect this may have on Darius. The road also had many potholes.

Loren said she did not have to worry yet because she was not that far along, and that this exercise would be good for her.

We finally found an extremely overpriced shop and bought what necessities we could find. We paid the exorbitant cost willingly to just not have to ride any further. We had all of the basic necessities and had even managed to pack some fish and beef between two bags of crushed ice.

The bicycles of course had big baskets on the handlebars. When we unloaded everything back at the cottage, we decided that we had done as much work as we wanted to do this day. We spent the rest of the day in very casual and slow-paced grown-up time.

We walked on our beach with the water up to our knees feeling like we were the only people on the planet. We admired the sunset and tossed our swimsuits onto the sand as we played in the shallow water. Suddenly I heard a sailboat tack and head back out into deeper water.

"Do you think they saw us?" Asked Loren.

"Oh yeah!" I said. "What the hell!!! They don't know who we are!" I pushed her out into deeper water, grabbed her around her arms, and dove into the next wave.

"AAaahhhh!!!" and the water fight was on!

We slept a lot. I think that our bodies were recharging from years of stress. We got so used to the stress that our bodies redefined it as normal. I forgot how good it felt to experience *this* . . .

We thoroughly enjoyed the rest of our time here on the island and even explored some of the ruins and other areas. There were a lot of tourist's things that we could have done but in general we just wanted to be together and left alone. Once again Momma Saborio knew what we needed, and with some strange power that I still don't understand managed to find this almost unknown island that we accidentally fell in love with months ago after a toss of a coin.

We called the driver and flew northwest from the Bight Airport. By the end of the day, we arrived at our house to find momma and both boys asleep on our bed. We left our luggage in the foyer and slipped into the kitchen for something cold to drink. We sat at the table as momma came in and wanted to know all about the cottage she rented. We told her as much about the vacation as she could handle hearing, and thanked her over and over for such a refreshing break. She told us that the boys were really missing us, and that is why they were sleeping on our bed.

Loren and I crept into the bedroom and crawled up onto the bed between the boys. We each put our arms around our sons and they rolled over against us without even waking up. We went to sleep too, and were anxious to see their expression when they woke up in our arms.

Momma went back to her private apartment and *probably* locked the door.

Four months later Loren was really starting to look pregnant. Her mood changes and her temper were considerably worse. We all knew that she was going through a hard time, and allowed her the free space to cope with it. This is her second child and they were both by me, so theoretically this pregnancy should be almost identical to the first one, so I thought. Momma came to me and told me that Loren did not have this much pain and cramping when she had David, and she was a little bit worried. She suggested that I have Loren checked out, but I could not get Loren to go with her increasingly grumpy attitude.

Over the next few months Loren got huge. She was having pain in her back as she had to lean backwards to stabilize her tummy weight. We both talked to Darius regularly to try to calm him down as he often pounded on her while she attempted to sleep. Sometimes she would be just fine walking around the house and other times I could not even make her get out of the bed in the morning.

As I watched the news, they were tracking a hurricane moving across all of my favorite sailing areas. I worried about my friends in St. Croix and was watching the spaghetti projections that showed the hurricane moving toward the Bahamas and possibly even the east coast of Florida. It had been raining on and off for several days now. The hurricane appeared to be staying offshore. Just in case, I went out to the boat and doubled the dock lines, spring lines, and borrowed some worn-out tires from the local tire store to use as padding against the sea wall. Regardless of whether it passed us or not, it still looked like we are going to take a beating.

I came back into the house and the news station was flashing the red warning across the top of the screen and still showing the same hypothetical projection of the hurricane's path. It was looking now like a direct hit into Miami and then turning north. It appeared to be headed straight up the middle. It was raining harder outside now and I rolled down the hurricane shutters while I still could. The cars were all in the garage and the garage doors came with hurricane bracing on the inside. I walked up to the bedroom and into the shower. I got into the bed carefully. Loren had already gone to sleep.

At about 2 AM Loren woke me up holding her tummy and told me the labor pains were getting too bad, and that she wanted to go to the hospital, NOW!

The palm trees were bending back and forth in the wind and branches were scattered all across the lawn and the driveway.

The boat was jerking back and forth on the spring lines and you could hear the tires squeaking as my beautifully waxed fiberglass smashed against the black rubber.

I helped Loren into her Land Rover. Momma watched from the hallway and told me to call her when I get there. I hit the garage door opener and the wind blew some plastic child's toys into the side of the car. I just backed out and closed the garage door fighting the wind and rain that made it almost impossible to see. It was a long drive just to get out of our subdivision and the nearest hospital was about 30 min. up Rt.1. When I got to the traffic light at Rt.76 there had been a traffic accident with a fatality, and traffic was backed up in all directions. I drove off into the grass and around the traffic jam while some angry people sitting in line, blew their horns at me.

Loren screamed . . . . so I hit the brakes and turned to help her. "Go!! Just GO!!" She yelled . . . I hit the gas and continued.

As I got closer to the intersection and was ready to turn onto Rt.1, a police car with flashing lights pulled in front of me and blocked my exit. I angrily jumped out into the torrential downpour and the officer jumped out of his car and pointed his 9 mm at me. I raised my hands up over my head immediately and screamed . . . .

"MY WIFE IS HAVING A BABY!"

His pistol went back into his holster.

"Follow me!"

He jumped back into his car and waited until I was on his back bumper.

He didn't break any speed limits but at least he kept moving, and following his flashing lights was easier than trying to see the road through this terrible storm. Trees were down, signs were down, and in most of the intersections the traffic lights were no longer working. The electric in the entire area was out. We drove through water in one area that came up to the bottom of my doors. We finally got onto some clear road and started moving at 40 or 50 mph. Someone in a red Ford F-150, came through the intersection at 70 mph and T-boned the officer that was leading us. I locked up my brakes and slid through the intersection as Loren screamed from the pain of the seat belt squeezing against her body. I continued through the intersection and pulled off to see if she was okay.

"My waters broke!" as she showed me her hand with a panicked look on her face.

I put the pedal on the floor and drove as fast as I safely could toward the hospital. I came around the next curve only to find another traffic accident with a semi-truck and there was no way to get around this one. I kissed Loren and told her I would be right back. I left the car and ran through the traffic jam toward another emergency medical van that had just arrived.

The driver of the semi-truck was okay and the driver of the car was dead. I quickly explained my emergency to the EMTs and two of them grabbed their bags and followed me back to my car. When we arrived, Loren's labor pains had intensified and she was in extreme pain. My adrenalin was peaked. I kept seeing a vision of Lisa in the bathtub as the EMT's laid her across the seat. He leaned into the car trying to shield her from the pummeling rain. There were pieces of sheet metal and tree branches flying through the air and smashing on cars around us. People were panicking and trying to turn around and go back where they came from.

"*PUSH!*" I heard the medic yell. I tried to see what he was doing but there was no room as the second medic tried to hold his raincoat over the first. I could barely see through the windshield. I saw Loren's stressed and wrinkled face trying to deal with the pain. *I had to help her* .... I wasn't there for Lisa .... I have to help her! ... I pressed against the glass as the medic yelled. My heart beat like a drum solo.

"*SIR!!!! ... SIR!!!*" And the drumming stopped. I ran around the car.

"YES!"

"*Congratulations!!! You have a daughter!*"

He smiled and let me see my daughter as tears rolled down my face. I was glad now that it was raining. The medic covered the baby, protecting her with his body, and headed for the van.

The first medic had gone back into the car to finish things with Loren. I relaxed and hung against the car door not feeling the rain or wind anymore.

I had a *DAUGHTER?* . . . He said?

Suddenly I heard Loren's scream breaking the silence.

"AAAAAAHHHH!!!!!!!"

I postponed my second heart attack.

The medic popped his head out of the car pulling the radio from his belt as he looked into my face concerned.

"Joe . . . . bring another birthing kit . . . we have a second one!"

He ducked back into the car.

I stood there confused. I was supposed to be getting a son named Darius. Instead I got a new daughter, and now I'm getting *another baby?*

I stepped back and looked at the car to make sure I brought the medics to the right one.

"*SIR!!!!*" He yelled, but I was already standing there.

"You've got another daughter!!!! *TWINS!!!!!*"

I almost hit the ground . . . In a few seconds, I forced my body off the hood of the car.

"How's Loren???" I asked, trying to see if there were any more surprises.

"She will be fine!! Just give us room to work sir!"

The emergency van pulled up with all lights flashing and stopped beside the car. The medic handed the second child to the driver. They put Loren on a gurney and covered her as they moved her into the back of the van. I slammed the doors on the Rover and hit the lock button. I ran to the van as the medic held the side door open for me.

As we drove toward the hospital with Loren holding a baby under each arm, I punched in the phone number at the house.

RRRrrrrring!!!!

HELLO . . . . Jonah????" Said momma with relief in her voice.

"Momma . . . Darius is . . . twins . . . girls!"

"I know."